PRINCE OF
WRATH

PRINCES OF SIN: SEVEN DEADLY SINS SERIES

K. ELLE MORRISON

This novel is a work of fiction. All characters and events portrayed are products of author's imagination and used fictitiously.
Editing by Caroline Acebo
Proofreading by Norma's Nook Proofreading
Cover Designed by Cassie Chapman at Opulent Designs
Interior page design by K. Elle Morrison

Kellemorrison.com

Copyright ©2023 K. Elle Morrison
All rights reserved. No part of this book may be reproduced or used in any manner without the prior written permission of the copyright owner, expect for the use of brief quotations in a book review.
Print ISBN: 979-8-9887063-9-7
Ebook ISBN: 979-8-9898130-0-1

For the J-named fuck boys.
Thanks for the trauma, and nights I wouldn't want to forget.

DEAR READERS

Please read carefully

This book contains material that may be considered inappropriate for readers under the age of 18.
These materials cover:
Elements of religious trauma, graphic violence & murder, alcohol, and language. Graphic sex between consenting adults.

OTHER TITLES BY K. ELLE MORRISON

Blood On My Name
Audiobook:
Blood On My Name

The Princes of Sin series:
Prince Of Lust
Prince Of Greed
Prince Of Sloth
Prince Of Pride
Prince Of Gluttony
Prince Of Envy
Prince Of Wrath

The Black Banners Series:
Under The Black Banners
Dagger Of Ash & Gold

To stay up-to-date on upcoming titles, bonus material, advanced reader opportunities, and so much more visit Kellemorrison.com to join the newsletter!

For all upcoming projects and updates from K. Elle Morrison please subscribe to the *FREE* Newsletter!

Kellemorrison.com
Linktree

How did you get this number?

I have my sources.

Send me a picture.

Did you lose your mind while I was gone?

Contract

[Name or Your Company's Name]
[ine 1]
[ine 2]
[Zip Code]

[Name or Company's Name]
[1]
[Code]

e or Heading

"Agreement") is made and entered into on [Date], between [Your Name or Company's Name] ("Party A") and or Company's Name] ("Party B").

e or objective of the agreement in cle...
ions:**

litions, and re...

CHAPTER 1
SLOANE

It had been eight years since I'd sold my soul to a devil. And not just any devil. A prince of Hell.

Eight years of living a truly unbelievable life that I had wished into existence and had worked hard to maintain. Endless nights of partying and days traveling to the farthest reaches of the globe had brought me more happiness and adventure than I could have ever imagined. I had seen and experienced life in ways that most people wouldn't have been prepared for.

What *I* hadn't prepared for was doing it alone.

Millions of dollars in my bank account. Homes in three different countries. Stocks in companies whose CEOs would have turned their noses up at me ten years ago.

All testaments to how far I had come in this life, and all things that didn't keep me warm at night.

The media would have the masses think that celebrity relationships were fleeting due to money or distance. But in my case, and several others I knew personally, relationships tended to end in volition due to the influence of Seere, Prince of Wrath.

My soul had been marked as his. That wasn't the only reason for my inability to keep a healthy affair alive, but his uncanny desire to be near me *had* ended several potential loves. Seere always found me, no matter how far I ran or whom I'd invited into my bed. It didn't matter how kind the person was when we started seeing each other. By the end, they were stark raving hellions.

It might have been eight years since I lost the only thing I'd ever truly owned to the demon, but it had only been two months since I'd last seen him. I thought I'd found a way to get him out of my life for good.

Yet there he was, watching me over the rim of his cup as a gorgeous man stared directly at my chest while telling me about his yacht and three Aston Martins.

A pool party raged around us, complete with a toxic, luxury drug scene.

The wealth of men hadn't interested me in years, but letting them brag got them harder than my lingerie did.

I had stopped listening long before Seere's dark green eyes had caught my attention from several yards away. Tonight, neither of us was alone. An otherworldly beautiful blond man was attempting to converse with Seere. His eyes pinged between me and the side of Seere's jaw. If I had to guess, I would say that man was also a demon. I couldn't think of a time when I had seen Seere speaking to anyone, and this stranger was comfortable with the intensity that radiated from Seere's body.

Any hope that Seere's companion would distract him long enough for me to slip away was smaller than the attention span I had for the human man burning holes through my dress with his eyes.

"So, what do you think, beautiful?" Todd's voice broke the visual tether between Seere and me.

"Oh sorry. The music is so loud. What was the question?"

Todd didn't skip a beat. Whatever he had planned clearly had more to do with my clothes coming off than with keeping my attention. "The dock is only down the hill. I'd love to take you out on the water for a moonlight tour. Then maybe we could lie out on the deck to look at the stars with some wine?"

I dared a quick glance back at Seere. Occupied, but not for long.

Leaving the pool party was a gamble, but one I was willing to take if it meant that I could escape a tongue lashing from my debtor prince.

"Sure. Lead the way." I smiled up at Todd, who looked surprised that someone had finally taken his bait.

"Uh, great. Let me just tell my buddy we're headed out. I was his ride." He scanned the crowd, but I hooked my hand into the crook of his arm and pulled him back.

"Send him a text," I said, sex laced through my words.

"Yes, ma'am."

Todd's yacht wasn't the largest in the marina, but as far as oversized boats went, it was nice and far from the shore. Todd stood at the helm, steering the boat out into calmer waters so we could drift smoothly. I had taken to the living room on the main deck to wait out my initial sea sickness. Once we were anchored, my stomach and nerves would settle.

The tips of my fingers itched at the hem of my short cocktail dress where a thin line of scripture was inked. A ward given to me by a man in Italy who claimed to be a specialist in demonic possession and the exorcism of dark forces. I had thought the etchings on my skin had worked. For months, Seere had stayed far away. Until tonight.

It could have been a coincidence. He could have very well been there to collect on someone else. If he'd wanted to corner me, he would have.

I told this to myself with each passing yard we put between ourselves and the shoreline.

Todd came bounding down the stairs and shuffled over to a line of cabinets. He grabbed two glasses and a bottle of wine and motioned for me to follow him back to the upper deck. I obliged, but the chill of the air whipping around us had me rethinking my willingness to spend the night on a boat on the Pacific Ocean.

Todd came to stand next to me after he dropped anchor. "Here, you must be cold." He shrugged off his jacket and hung it over my shoulders.

"Thanks." I slipped my arms into the sleeves and wrapped the fabric around myself.

"We'll head to the main deck in a few minutes, but I really wanted to show you how clear the sky was out here," he said, looking up. "The stars are incredible this far from the city lights."

"It's beautiful," I agreed with a sigh.

"Not as beautiful as you are." He delivered the cheesy line and wrapped his arm around my waist. "Let's take this party below deck."

I leaned into him and brushed my lips over his. A

small wanton hum vibrated between us, and he answered with a whine of pleasure.

Back in the warmth of the main deck, Todd led me over to the inset sectional couch then pulled me onto his lap. His thin mouth worked mine as his hands roamed over my body and up my dress. His erection gouged into my hip as he maneuvered me onto my back and settled between my legs. The white leather under me squeaked and rubbed at my now-bare ass as he pushed the hem of my dress up past my waist.

He paused to look at me, lust and hunger in his hazel eyes as they trailed from my thong to my chest and back down. The tattoo on my thigh caught his attention, and he passed a finger over the letters.

"You're a bad girl, aren't you?" He grinned. "Where else do you have ink?" I assumed he meant for that question to be seductive.

"Just the one. It's sort of like . . . protection," I explained.

"We won't need any of that tonight, baby. I got snipped years ago."

I internally cringed but was also surprised by his admission. Men rarely took precautions into their own hands, especially ones I knew, but I doubted the intention behind it was admirable.

"Can't have any of my boys making the journey for free. This is prime real estate." He gestured at his crotch then began to undo his pants. I assumed to show me his desirable property.

"That's . . . uh." I was speechless.

Actually, I wasn't. But it was probably best that I kept my mouth closed.

"I'm about to rock your world, baby. Are you ready for me?"

My teeth tugging on my bottom lip was answer enough for him. He descended on me like a wolf on a lost sheep. Teeth and saliva made a line from my jaw to the middle of my chest before two of his long fingers pushed my panties out of his way and jammed inside of me.

"You're so wet for me." He was obviously clueless as to how wet a woman could really get if she were aroused.

The boat jerked and threw him to the ground. "What the hell was that?" With a curse of pain, he got to his knees and headed to the stairs leading to the cockpit.

Left half naked on the couch, I sat up and righted my clothes through the gnawing dread in my chest.

I knew what Hell had rocked the boat.

And it was here for me.

How did you get this number?

I have my sources.

Send me a picture.

Did you lose your mind while I was gone?

Contract

e or Your Company's Name]
e 1]
e 2]
ip Code]

me or Company's Name]

Code]

 or Heading**

greement") is made and entered into on [Date], between [Your Na...
r Company's Name] ("Party B").

or objective of the agreement in cle... ...pany's Name] ("Party A") and

ons:**

tions, and res... ...terms,

CHAPTER 2
SEERE

Sloane had been running from me. Rightfully so. She was my crown jewel this millennium. Smart. Driven. Cunning. Beautiful.

She hadn't just asked for fame, riches, or a lush life. She wanted power.

When Sloane summoned me, she wanted to have the knowledge and connections to build an empire. No other human who had called upon me had already planned how they would keep the gifts I gave them, but she had. She'd also had a score to settle.

Her ex was a pro hockey player turned sports attorney. She had followed Ben around the country for years. She gave him comfort. Forgave him for the nights he was unfaithful. Tolerated drunken rants that ended with her in tears and covered in bruises.

When he finally got bored, he dropped her faster

than a puck to ice. But Ben hadn't just dumped her, he exiled her. Changed the locks to the apartment they'd shared, abandoned her in a city with no money, no job, no way back to her family. Most would have asked for his life to be taken, but not Sloane.

No.

My little spitfire wanted to crush him. And she had, easily. She became the most successful agent the NHL had ever seen, and only in partial thanks to my influence. She had a natural eye for up-and-comers. But with her charm and intelligence, she was a killer in negotiations. She had surpassed her peers and had racked up sums of money that other humans would kill for.

Though the company she kept had never been worthy of her, tonight was too much to stomach.

The trust-fund nepo baby she had drooling over her had been given everything on a gold platter. His father was a wealthy television executive who had paid Todd's way through college and had given him a prime job with plenty of underlings to make decisions for him. But Todd's biggest fault was that he had his fingers inside of what was mine.

I watched him scurry up the stairs, and then Sloane stood to pull her dress down. Her heart was pounding so loud for me that I knew she could feel my presence. Closing the distance, I wound my fingers around the loose curls at her back. Once she registered the gentle tug on her silken strands, she froze.

"Did you miss me?" I whispered, bringing her into my chest.

Her breathing quickened. "What do you want, Seere?"

I buried my nose in her hair. Coconut, lime, and gin filled my lungs. She shuddered against me.

"It's been too long since you last checked in, Sloane. Your mortal life is so short, you know. It would be a shame for me to not be present for too much of it."

"You've found me. Now leave before Todd comes back and you lose control again."

Her ferocity and scathing tone roused me in more ways than one.

"Do you like this one?" I asked, reaching a hand up to her chin and directing her face toward the stairs. "Because I don't think he's good enough for you."

"According to you, no one is."

She was right.

There wasn't a human alive good enough for her. And seeing her leave with that lowlife had grated on my last nerve.

"He can't fulfill you," I said into the column of her neck. The words raised goose bumps on her skin. "That fire inside of you would be smothered to cinders in his hands."

The sounds of footsteps coming down the stairs pulled her attention away.

"I'm not sure what hit us, but we're going to have to take his party back to sh—" Todd's eyes bulged at the sight of another man's hands on the woman he had claimed for the night. "Who the fuck are you?"

The challenge in his voice twisted my lips. Sloane tried to step out of my hold, but my hand slipped from her neck to her chest, holding her still.

"Why don't you introduce me to your friend, my little flame?"

Her heart thrashed against her sternum.

"All right, asshole," Todd said, "I don't know who you are or how you got on the boat but—"

"But what? What are you going to do to me, Todd?" I stepped around Sloane and slipped my hands into the pockets of my slacks. "Are you going to punch me? Finally use that semester of boxing lessons you took in boarding school?"

His face contorted in confusion. "How . . . How would you . . ."

The puzzle of who I was and where I had come from was too much for coherent sentences.

He watched me as I made a slow, deliberate path around him. Once, then twice.

"I know more than that, Todd," I finally answered. "I

know you steal money from your father's firm. And that when you were twelve, you convinced one of your sister's friends to take off her pants so you could play doctor."

Every sin he'd committed came flowing through me in quick succession. Flashes of women he'd raped after feeding them shots at the fraternity house. Dozens, if not more. Every misdeed down to unpaid parking tickets until the moment his fingers had entered my territory.

"Does your fiancée know you stole then sold her mother's engagement diamond before replacing it with glass? Or better yet, does she know that you've cheated on her thirteen times this year? It would have been more, but you're not as charming as you perceive yourself to be. Isn't that right, darling?"

I shot a look at Sloane, whose horrified expression was fixed on the man who had prodded her cunt only minutes ago.

I walked another circle around him. "By the way, can you tell me the name of your gorgeous date tonight? You've really outdone yourself this time. She's quite the catch."

"I—her name is, uh . . ." His eyes darted between Sloane and me, which gave him the appearance of a rat trapped on a sinking ship.

"You've got to be kidding me. You don't even know

my name?" Sloane finally broke her silence. Anger flared her nostrils, and fire burned in her eyes.

"It's just . . . I didn't catch it when you told me at the party. It was so loud, and I was tipsy."

Sloane shook her head in her disgust.

I returned to Sloane's side and slipped my arm around her waist. "To answer your question, I am a demon, and I am here to deliver punishment for your wicked ways."

Her eyes shot to me, but the ball of dark, heavy energy was already growing in my free hand. I held it up for Todd to inspect before allowing it to fall through the floor, crackling and popping with the melting of steel and plastic. The hull whined and sizzled until the vessel started taking on water. But before Todd could release his first terrified screech, I pulled Sloane through the void and into the front room of her Malibu home.

She leaped from my hold.

"Fuck!" She fisted her hair. "I left my purse. My phone is in there. I have to call the Coast Guard. He could die. Damn it, Seere!"

I held up my hand, her purse dangling on two of my fingers. "Don't worry, spitfire. He found the life vests and raft. Unlike the female form, he knows his way around that boat."

Sloane snatched her purse and rummaged through

it to find her phone, but the battery was dead. I'd made sure of that.

"You've gone too far this time." She coughed out through tears of relief. Or maybe frustration.

I closed the distance between us, backing her up until I was the only thing she could see.

My hand on the wall near her head caged her into my torso. "You needed a reminder of who you belonged to, Sloane."

I dragged the tips of my fingers up her thigh, and the palm of my hand nudged the hem of her dress up to reveal her tattoo. A ugly mark that was not only put there by someone other than me, but it had made my life tedious for far too long.

"You've become too comfortable running from me." My eyes fell between us to the ink. Her gaze followed and she watched as the dark lines lightened then disappeared. "There now. Isn't that better?"

"It's not like it worked anyway," she said with a sardonic huff, daggers staring back at me when our eyes met.

"It was harder to find you, but you can never run far enough from me."

My hand at her thigh inched higher, and her breaths quickened as I hooked a finger into the seam of her panties.

"The hunt was thrilling, but knowing that I can

touch you anytime I want . . ."

"Seere." The warning in her breathy voice stilled my exploring digits.

"I love the sound of my name on your tongue. Can I have a taste?" I teased her bottom lip with a slow lick.

For the quickest of moments, I thought I could feel her jaw relax as if she were contemplating letting me in. The crack in the iron wall she had built around herself gave me a glimpse of my truest desire. But it faded as soon as it had started.

She gasped, and her hand gripped my wrist. The fear that staunched her face attempted to hide the race of daring in her veins. With a tender touch, I could coax the lust from the depths she was shoving it into. I could have her moaning my name and begging for mercy.

But not tonight.

Not with the scent of another man still so fresh on her skin.

I opened the space between our bodies, but she didn't let go of my arm. Her anger had slipped into surprise, maybe even longing. And that was how I would leave her.

Wanting.

Loathing.

Craving.

"I'll be seeing you soon, Sloane."

Contract

[Your Name or Your Company's Name]
[Address Line 1]
[Address Line 2]
[City, State, Zip Code]

[Their Name or Company's Name]
[Address]

[Zip Code]

Title or Heading

This Agreement ("Agreement") is made and entered into on [Date], between [Your Name or Company's Name] ("Party A") and [Their Name or Company's Name] ("Party B").

Purpose or objective of the agreement in clear terms.

Definitions:

definitions, and

CHAPTER 3
SLOANE

Seere vanished before my eyes, a trick he really seemed to enjoy performing, considering I couldn't remember him ever entering or leaving a room through a doorway. The knot in my stomach accompanied me to my bedroom, where my phone charger was plugged in next to my bed.

My phone was my lifeline. Every appointment was booked on my calendar. Hundreds of contacts and even more social media connections lived in my pocket—or, more realistically, in my hand. I was rarely out of contact with my assistant and never unavailable to my clients. For the last six seasons, I'd been the agent for several of the top NHL players, so I didn't get much sleep.

When the screen lit up, I only had a handful of

missed notifications, but the one I looked at first was from my best friend that I'd been with at the party.

> **MAXIE**
>
> You're not going to believe what happened after you left with that cutie.

Maxine loved drama and lived for these sorts of reports. I scrolled to the solid paragraph that recapped her night.

> **MAXIE**
>
> First, there was some chick wandering around, looking for the owner of that exclusive bar we went to last week. I guess he knew someone at the party, but she claims to have fucked him in the DJ booth. I didn't see him there, but she went on and on about how huge his dick was. Anyway, not even twenty minutes later, there's some crazy commotion out in the water. Like, a whole ass boat sank! Then, while everyone was outside, trying to see the wreck, some guy FELL OFF THE CLIFF! HE DIED!
>
> Can you believe it?
>
> Sloane?
>
> Bitch, you better answer me!

> **SLOANE**
>
> Holy shit. That's wild!

I typed my response quickly, but my gut clenched. Now I knew who that blond guy talking to Seere was.

It was Sitri. Fuck. What had Sitri been doing there?

I couldn't blame the woman who had been searching for him at the party. Seere had first introduced me to him years ago, when we'd visited The Deacon. He was so sexy and charismatic. It had been easy to get lost in his smile. Seere had threatened to take me right there on the dance floor to remind me that I was his and he wouldn't be sharing.

Classic possessive Prince of Wrath.

MAXIE

> I know! BTW, if you didn't answer in the next five minutes, I was going to report it to the sexy cop who's blocking off the LITERAL CRIME SCENE

SLOANE

> Are you saying that guy falling wasn't an accident?

MAXIE

> No one knows anything. We're all still trying to get ride services to clear out, but he told that crazy dick-loving chick that he felt like he was being watched. Creepy, right?

SLOANE

> So creepy. But you're okay?

MAXIE

Yeah. I'm good. Ashton is giving me a ride home.

SLOANE

Oh God. No. I'll come get you. Don't go home with your ex . . . again.

MAXIE

Come get me? Where are you?

SLOANE

I'm home. It didn't happen with Todd. He's a jerk.

MAXIE

Well, shit. Don't hate me, but one of us should get laid tonight and I vote that it's me.

I rolled my eyes. Ashton had led Maxine on for years. He'd promised to marry her every couple months, but the ring never came. Then he'd started ghosting her for trips with "the boys" up to Napa or out to Vegas, where he'd clearly fuck around on her. Once, he and his friends had gone to Brazil and he'd come back with dozens of photos on his phone of a woman he'd gotten naked.

SLOANE

Use protection. Never know where that dog's been lately.

MAXIE

Duh, I'm not that stupid. Last thing I need is a disease.

SLOANE

Or a parasite.

MAXIE

Plan B, baby!

SLOANE

Maxie!

MAXIE

JK! I have plenty of condoms. MOM.

SLOANE

Love you. Call me tomorrow.

Maxie

XOXO

I moved on to my next notification. It was the lawyer for my newest client, a newbie who had been scouted during his junior year of high school and had played through college.

JIM

Kai got another offer on the table. I'm not interested but knew you'd want to know who put it in.

He forwarded me the email. The signature felt like a punch to my gut.

Benjamin Tremblay.

My hands were shaking. I put my phone face down on my nightstand. I couldn't answer yet. Nothing good would come from my giving Jim my first reaction to that news. Hot, angry tears filled my eyes for the second time in less than an hour. The two men responsible colliding once again on the same night was too coincidental.

Ben dragged my heart all over three countries for the better part of two years. We'd met at college during a game. He was a hockey player; I was covering the away game for the school paper. I fell for him harder than a center taking lumber.

When Ben left me stranded in Phoenix, Arizona, with no way back to Toronto, I called the only person I thought would answer. Rick Donnelly was the goalie for Ben's team and had always said things to me in passing that made me wonder if he'd always known Ben was a piece of shit.

That phone call changed my life.

Rick offered not only to let me crash at his place—and gave up his bed for me—but he offered to call Seere to see if he could help me. He also paid me to care for his exotic fish while he traveled for games.

Turned out that as a young rookie, Rick had made a deal with Seere to get into the NHL with a full contract. Overnight, Rick was connected to one of the best agents at the time and was signed within the week.

I'd refused his offer to meet Seere at first.

My plan was to apply to all the schools I could with a new major in mind: sports law and management. I had been in the last year of my environmental law degree when Ben was recruited. He'd caught a scout's eye during one of his last senior games. He was a lazy player and relied on his supports to score. Going pro hadn't been in his plans, but when the opportunity to make millions of dollars a year fell into his lap, he took it.

Weeks after moving in with Rick, I had been rejected from every university I'd applied to. I was still too broke to get a ticket back to Canada. During a night of sad drinking, I asked Rick about Seere, and the devilish asshole showed up in a blink of an eye.

Much like he had tonight, he turned my world upside down and left me feeling like a stone had sunk in my gut. Seere knew things about me that no one else should. The intrusiveness of his ability was like someone finding your diary from the sixth grade and reciting it at a poetry slam. Embarrassing. Mortifying. Defrocking.

Then his attention shifted. The first time he'd done this, I was so surprised that I'd easily fallen under his spell. Every promise he gave filled me deeply.

"You want him to suffer."

I did.

"You want your name to outshine his in his own field."

I was starved for it.

"You want him to never feel satisfaction with anyone else—or himself—for the rest of his miserable life."

That was everything I could have ever wanted and more. And Seere had granted those wishes without hesitation.

What more could a woman want than a man who did exactly what he said he would, especially when the world was full of ones who never fulfilled their promises?

Through the years, Seere had done things to my mind and body that ruined me. Sex, like everything else he did, was both rough and sensual. Enthralling and debilitating. With every gasp he drew out of me, he injected his darkness to replace it until he'd dragged me so far into the deep end that I didn't need the light to survive. I only needed him.

The withdrawals I lived through were devastating and eventually pushed me to find ways to banish him from my life entirely. He owned my soul, but that didn't mean he had the rights to my life or body.

I thought I'd finally settled into a life without Seere. I hadn't seen or heard from him in months. And now I was left wondering why he and Ben had both found their ways back to me on the same night and what the next day would bring.

How did you get this number?

I have my sources.

Send me a picture.

Did you lose your mind while I was gone?

Contract

e or Your Company's Name]
e 1]
e 2]
ip Code]

me or Company's Name]

Code]

or Heading**

greement") is made and entered into on [Date], between [Your Na... ...pany's Name] ("Party A") and
r Company's Name] ("Party B").

or objective of the agreement in clea...

ns:**

ions, and ... ...terms.

CHAPTER 4
SEERE

Sloane meant more to me than just another soul or notch on my headboard. Being inside of her gave me more than pleasure; it gave me existence. Heaven above and Hell below were for nothing if I wasn't thrusting deep inside of her, making her moan my true name in ragged, spent breaths until we both collapsed from exhaustion.

When she'd inked that fucking ward on her skin, I felt my connection to her soul deaden. It hadn't disappeared. She could never sever it completely. Even in death. Especially in death. But the clear sight I usually had on her had blurred like looking through a foggy window onto a hazy morning.

I knew she couldn't run forever. She needed me. She never would admit it, but she needed *me*. Chasing her to the ends of the Earth only intensified my hunger, and finally laying my eyes on her tonight had brought me back to a time when I didn't have boundaries.

After the Fall, I'd been merciless. Destroying lives and empires had been an insatiable thirst that only the blood of thousands fulfilled.

That was the need I felt bubbling to the surface tonight.

How beautiful Sloane would look painted in blood and ash. With my ass firmly planted on my throne, she would be my crown.

But she'd run. I had to remember that. She would come to me on her own eventually.

So I would wait. I wasn't the most patient demon. By my own admission and faults, I would rather sift through rubble for what I desired than wait for the statue to weather to my will. But Sloane was worth every agonizing moment, and I could feel that our time apart was coming to an end.

With more frustration than I cared to admit and my lungs full of her scent, I traveled through the void back home. To my surprise, the lights were all on downstairs.

When Vassago returned from his entrapment, my brother moved into my spare bedroom. His former home had long since been demolished due to misuse and decay. He'd surely get another soon, but I liked having him around. Before he'd disappeared for fifty years, we'd been inseparable.

I came into the kitchen to find him flipping through one of the cookbooks my designer had placed on a stand for aesthetics.

"I know a chef or two if you're hungry."

His head popped up. Either he hadn't heard me step through the void or he hadn't expected me to be home yet. To be honest, I hadn't expected him this early. He'd been out all day and night, pursuing his newest obsession.

"Do humans still eat that terrible Jell-O casserole?" He wrinkled his nose and looked at the pages he was thumbing through.

"Thank Satan, no. They've moved on to replacing meat with soy and nutmeats though." I opened the fridge and pulled out a container of the prepped dinner my chef had made at the beginning of the week.

"Nutmeat? What does that mean?"

"They milk them too and use it in their coffee instead of cow or goat milk."

He shut the book with a snap. "For the sake of all the fucking holy." He sounded exhausted and annoyed at the world.

"We don't talk about them in this house." I shook my head and wagged my finger mockingly. "No need to invite the unwanted."

I brought down two plates from the cupboard and offered one to him.

He raised a brow and took the plate. "Tabamiah doesn't drop in on you anymore?"

"Not since I threatened to destroy them when they appeared at the foot of my bed when I had two models in it."

He watched as I placed the prepped meal in the microwave. His cheekbones matched my own and his dark hair was a shade lighter, but that was all we had in common. His tall, broad build and chiseled jawline made him look more sinister. Not that it was the wrong impression, after all.

"I haven't seen Syrael since I was freed. Not sure if that's a blessing or a sign of something yet to come."

Our constraining angels used to have shorter leashes. I wasn't surpassed that Syrael hadn't shown himself. The prince he had been instructed to monitor had gone missing. What sort of guard dog let their one and only charge slip away undetected?

I pulled a bottle of wine from the small fridge below the counter and unscrewed the top before pouring two glasses. "You have enough to worry about. Father's favorites do as well."

"Are the angels busier this end of the century?" He took a long sip and savored it in his cheeks before swallowing.

"Even less so. Wherever their focus lies in the

universe, it isn't here." I lifted my glass. "And thank fuck for that."

I finished my wine in one gulp.

After the microwave timer went off, I served the pasta, asparagus, and chicken cutlets then poured the white wine sauce over our portions. Vassago watched me take my first bite then gathered a similar arrangement on his own fork. A bite-sized piece of chicken, the top of an asparagus, then wrapping it with sauce drenched spaghetti.

The lines on his face morphed as each flavor profile hit his senses until he swallowed and smiled down to his plate.

"The food has improved. What is this?" Vassago took another big mouthful.

"Chicken Bianco," I answered between bites. "The food industry has vastly grown since you've been away."

He looked around at the mansion. "Many things have."

I didn't have such a large home half a century ago. Not that I couldn't, but I hadn't decided whether I was going to stay in the country. I'd planned on going back to Europe, but with the vacuum of a prince missing, one abdicating his duties, and another fleeing to the deserts of the Southwest, I'd had to stay put. Sitri, Orobas, and Stolas had begged for me to stay. They'd worried I would find myself in more trouble than they could handle when the means of communication were dependent on wires and stamps.

If I had gone, I wouldn't have acquired Sloane. What a shame that would have been. To have never tasted her supple flesh or filled my hands with her soft curves.

It would have been a waste of a lifetime to never have fucked her sweet pussy.

I wonder if she's still awake?

"Thanks for dinner, but I have to go. Celeste should be out of her study session. I need to be sure she makes it home."

Vass' worried face pulled my head out of a dangerous thought.

"Celeste is a grown woman. She can get home without an escort."

His eyes snapped to mine, and the raw anger in them was enough for me to butt out of his affairs.

"Sorry. Go. I'll see you tomorrow." I waved him off, but he had vanished before I'd finished my statement.

The house was still again.

Was there irony in being jealous of the Prince of Envy?

Not only that he had found a woman worth living for but that she seemed to enjoy his attention. Their budding relationship was blooming too slowly for my own liking, but then again, I hadn't wasted any time getting Sloane into bed after we'd made our deal.

It hadn't been hard. She was obvious with her affection at first, squirming under my lingering gaze, wearing undergarments in my favorite color and letting them show when I found an excuse to be around her.

Though I'd never told her, it wasn't in my nature to make myself known in such an intimate way to the souls I bartered. She was special. The fire in her spoke to me. Watching how the fuel I provided to her spite facilitated her growth had been one of my favorite entertainments.

Ben had been forced to stand in her shadow to witness her transformation, but he was in the cheap nosebleeds. I'd had a bedside seat for the show.

I cleared my plate, rinsed it in the sink, then headed up the stairs to my bedroom. My reunion with Sloane had ended with a lot less skin than I'd craved. A cold shower and pleasuring myself wouldn't take the burden of being unsated.

I took my phone out of my pocket and opened a new text thread with the phone number I'd taken before killing Sloane's cell phone battery.

UNKNOWN NUMBER

> I can't get the taste of your lips out of my head. When can I have another?

SLOANE

How did you get this number?

UNKNOWN NUMBER

I have my sources.

Send me a picture.

SLOANE

Did you lose your mind while I was gone?

UNKNOWN NUMBER

Yes. And I've lost all memory of what your tits look like.

Remind me.

SLOANE

Fuck you.

UNKNOWN NUMBER

Is that an invitation?

Because there are several ways I would do just that.

SLOANE

You sank a damn boat tonight! Do you really think I'm in the mood for your flirting?

UNKNOWN NUMBER

I was under the impression you were in the mood to fuck me.

SLOANE

I'm going to bed. Don't text me.

UNKNOWN NUMBER

You're right. Forgive me.

SLOANE

No way in Hell.

UNKNOWN NUMBER

Are you sure about that? I bet I could make you forgive me.

SLOANE

Make me?

UNKNOWN NUMBER

Gladly.

SLOANE

Seere, I swear if you show up here, I will stab you!

UNKNOWN NUMBER

That's a little rougher than I like but depending on what you're wearing, I could get into it.

SLOANE

Stop.

I'm going to sleep.

Delete my number.

UNKNOWN NUMBER

Not a chance.

How did you get this number?

I have my sources.

Send me a picture.

Did you lose your mind while I was gone?

Contract

e or Your Company's Name]
ne 1]
ne 2]
Zip Code]

ame or Company's Name]
1]
']
Code]

e or Heading**

Agreement") is made and entered into on [Date], between [Your Name or Company's Name] ("Party A") and or Company's Name] ("Party B").

e or objective of the agreement in clea

ons:**

itions, and re   terms.

CHAPTER 5
SLOANE

The next morning, I got to the office earlier than normal. With the email that Jim had shown me, I knew there would be more fires to put out, and I was right.

Chloe, my junior agent, came bustling toward me with her phone wedged between her cheek and shoulder, another phone held out to me, and her other arm full of documents.

"I'm so sorry. I know I should have called you sooner, but you said not to bother you before seven a.m.—especially on Pilates mornings—though I did get your coffee and breakfast order ready and at your desk. Anyway, Jose called and—"

"Chloe." I held up my hands and locked eyes with her. "Breathe. In"—we took a long inhale together—"and out."

She blew hers out in a rush then waited for me to speak.

"I will call Jose back. Who is on the other line?"

"Marco, Ralf's assistant."

"Tell him that I'll also call him back after we've had our morning all-hands." I turned to my assistant, Lora, and waved her over. "Now, did you eat?"

"Yes," Chloe answered.

"Good." I turned to Lora, who had a guilty look on her face. "Did you eat?"

She shrugged sheepishly. "I was running late."

"Bagels," I said. "From Broker in West."

She nodded and turned back to her desk to grab her purse.

"On the company card," I called after her. "And fill up your tank while you're out!"

I focused on Chloe again. "Which fire needs to be put out first?"

"Jose. He got a call from an agent who wants to turn him. He's thinking about taking it because the guy promised him a 'mil more per season.'"

My blood was already boiling. Jose had been a hard sell to begin with, and I'd not only gotten him the trade he'd wanted for over a year, but I'd gotten him more money than he'd asked for. The fact that he was willing to replace me only seven months into our contract was ridiculous.

With Chloe at my heels, I walked to my office and sat at my desk before I started dialing Jose's number. I pulled up our contract on my laptop and waited for him to answer.

"Hey, baby doll." His sickly sweet voice filled my ear.

"Morning, Jose." I laid it on just as thick as he had. "What's going on?"

"I didn't mean to scare your receptionist, but I know how hard you work for me when I light a fire under that perfect ass of yours."

I cringed at this sort of asshole mentality. Jose was hot, and he knew it too well. He'd slept with every woman interviewer, consultant, hairdresser, and manicurist that worked around him. He was a beauty on and off the ice.

"Your contract is locked in at $7.5 million, Jose. Another million would mean negotiations with a team who didn't need you. You've been riding pine for two games in a row. Don't think I don't watch."

"Ouch, doll." He feigned a hurt ego. "There's nothing wrong with trying. Besides, he said you'd beg for me to stay, and I would love to hear you beg."

"You've had your fun and made Chloe sweat. The next time you're bored, buy a puppy because I will drop you and let the wolves descend. You'll have your pick of the second-rate agents who would settle for $5 mil and half the endorsements."

"You're such a stone-cold tenner, Sloane. I love it when you boss me around." His sleazy side was coming out too comfortably. "Fine. Fine. You win. I'll tell this dude to fuck off, but I want to see you in the VIPs during the next game."

"Get off the bench and I'll be there."

He hollered with laughter, and I hung up.

Chloe stood in my doorway, clutching a stack of contracts. Her shoulders were hunched up to her ears, and I could see the stress building on her face.

Ben had found every single client I held or was hunting and had sent them an offer. I didn't know if he was planning to actually take them on, but what I did know was that he wanted to throw me into chaos while he made a larger move.

I had to get ahead of whatever that move was.

I took a calming breath and a sip of the coffee that Chloe had put on my desk. I knew what I had to do, but first, I had at least four more calls to make.

"Who's next?"

UNKNOWN NUMBER

I want to see you. Come to The Red Room.

THE TEXT LIT my phone screen while I was on a call to another agent who had also been hit by Hurricane Ben.

"No, I don't think he is going to take any more of your contracts. He's a shark. Don't drop blood in the water," I said but tuned out whatever Victor was saying on the other line.

SLOANE

Why?

UNKNOWN NUMBER

Have lunch with me.

SLOANE

I'm not eating lunch at a strip club like a 45-year-old divorced woman.

UNKNOWN NUMBER

That's a painful stereotype, and Gina is a great lady. She's really putting herself out there.

Proud of her.

Victor sighed in my ear. "Where did this guy even come from?"

I tapped my fingers on my phone keyboard while I answered both him and Seere. "Vancouver originally.

But the bastard got an extended work visa, it would seem."

SLOANE
Tell Gina to enjoy her lunch alone.

Seere hated men more than most women did. When he opened his lesbian strip club downtown, women had flocked to work there and later to partake in the entertainment.

Somehow, he had made it one of the most successful strip clubs in Los Angeles.

Victor continued to ramble. "But he can't just come here and sweep our rosters. What's the board going to think?"

"I don't know, but we are going to log an official complaint, and by the end of the week, hopefully something will come of it. The damage is done and that's all we can do right now." Another notification from Seere's incognito number popped up again. "Listen, Victor. Lunch next week and we can hash this all out. Okay?"

UNKNOWN NUMBER
I will after you meet me for a coffee.

SLOANE
Why do you want to see me?

"Okay, Sloane. I know you're feeling secure in all

this, but I've lost three of my best players already. I'm going to have to start scouting the fucking universities again!"

> UNKNOWN NUMBER
>
> I'll tell you in ten minutes. The coffee shop across the street from your office.

I rolled my eyes and set down my phone.

"Victor. You're being ridiculous." It was my turn to sigh. "Fight for your players. Lunch next week. I have to run."

Victor bid me goodbye, and we hung up. He wasn't a good agent to begin with, but he was easy to make a trade with, so I kept our professional relationship friendly.

"Lora," I called out. A moment later, my assistant was at my door. "I'm going to run out for a coffee."

"I can do that, Sloane." She quickly turned to start walking to her desk.

I had already grabbed my purse and was headed toward the door by the time she looked up again.

"I just need a break, and so do you," I said from the elevator, holding the door for her.

"Oh. Okay." She clambered inside beside me, and we rode to the first floor.

"Are you okay?" she asked gently.

45

I pulled her into a one-armed hug. "We're going to be fine. We aren't like the rest, remember?"

She nodded and smiled. "We're the best team a player could have."

We exchanged another smile and went our separate ways.

Contract

ne or Your Company's Name]
_ine 1]
ine 2]
Zip Code]

Name or Company's Name]
1]
2]
Code]

le or Heading**

"Agreement") is made and entered into on [Date], between [Your Na... ...pany's Name] ("Party A") and
or Company's Name] ("Party B").

e or objective of the agreement in clea...

tions:**

ditions, and ... ...erms,

CHAPTER 6
SEERE

Sloane crossed the street wearing a sexy pencil skirt and loose-fitting blouse. Lace from something sexy she had on underneath peeked behind the buttons she had undone. I wondered if she'd worn it just for me.

Her eyes found me in an instant.

I held up my hand and dipped my fingers to the seat across from mine. I'd already ordered for her.

She rolled her shoulders back, building herself up, then came to sit at the table with me.

"I'm here. What do you want?"

I nudged the saucer holding her cup closer to her. "It's lovely to see you too, little flame. Vanilla latte with whole milk and one sugar. Low foam. With whip."

She perked a brow at me and eyed the drink.

"We're in public. I didn't roofie it," I added.

"Wouldn't put it past you to try," she quipped but picked up the mug and took a sip.

Her lip dipped into the frothed milk, covering the ruby lipstick with a lickable layer of bubbles. She swiped her tongue across them slowly, aware of my eyes.

"Thanks." She placed her cup on its saucer and crossed her arms. "Tell me why you followed me on the boat last night and why you're sitting in a café across the street from my office."

"You're my favorite toy, and when I want to see what is mine, I will do so," I said simply.

"Why is Ben calling all my clients?" she shot back.

"I wouldn't know."

"Is that right?"

I nodded.

"Then I guess we're done here." She looked over at her purse and her brow perked as if she were going to attempt to leave.

As though I would allow that.

"Sit." The low command in my voice caused her to pause.

"Make me."

"We both know I will." I raised my brow and waited.

She eyed me, probably contemplating how far I would go to follow through on that threat in the middle of a human-infested coffee shop. Whatever she decided came with a huff, but she sat back down again like the good girl she was.

"What else do you have to say if it's not about the asshole you let weasel his way back to life?" Her words held more intensity than before.

"Why did you run from me?"

We'd been more involved than we'd ever been before she left for Europe for two months. When I realized she'd disappeared from my bed and left the country, I'd been more than enraged. The whole left wing of the house had to be rebuilt from the blast. It had taken weeks to catch up to her, but by then, she'd already found the man who'd inked her skin to ward her from me.

"I needed space." She lifted her chin.

"Cute." The sarcasm earned me a raise of her shoulder and a flip of her hair. "Knock off the vague little brat act."

"Make me—"

"If you keep saying 'Make me,' we're going to find out if I can make you the mother of my demon spawn. I'm sure if I fill that delicious cunt up with enough of my cum, something will grow."

Her jaw dropped and her hand flew up to cover it, but I'd gotten the reaction I wanted from her. She looked around, likely to see if anyone was eavesdropping on our salacious conversation, before she fixed me with a hard stare.

"I must really be getting under your skin, Seere." Her lips quirked. "It usually takes more than that to get you riled up."

"Having to hunt you through Europe and then through LAX has put me on edge. But now that you've come back to where you belong, I would like to ensure it stays that way."

She'd been back in L.A. for all of two weeks before I'd gotten wind of it. The party where I'd found her had been one of her first outings from what I could tell. What was bothering me the most was that she was acting as if nothing had happened.

"Answer me, Sloane." I reached under the table and gripped her knee gently.

The small two top gave me just enough room to glide my hand up her thigh to the hem of her skirt.

She slapped her hand over on mine. "This is why I left." The pressure of her hand lifted, and I snatched her fingers. "It was all too much."

I pulled our linked fingers over the tabletop then guided her knuckles to my lips. She watched as if I were a snake, ready to strike.

"Don't do that again, Sloane." Our eyes locked. "Or the next time I find you, it'll be more than a tiny boat that ends in wreckage."

She didn't agree. But she didn't refuse either. For Sloane, that was enough.

I moved on to more pressing matters. "From what I hear, you need a date to an affair tomorrow night?"

I would keep her close to me if Ben was—as she'd said—sniffing around.

"How did—never mind. No. I don't. I already have a date." She cautiously pulled her hand out of mine. I allowed it.

"I'll give you the rest of the day to change your mind." I took my phone out of my pocket and sent a text without blocking the number. "Send me a photo of what you're planning to wear. I would hate not to match."

I got to my feet with my takeaway cup in hand. She bolted up to stop me from leaving.

"Seere—"

I cupped the back of her neck and gave her a swift kiss. Not long enough to make a scene, but just enough to feel her lips meld to mine.

"Goodbye, little flame."

I left and was barely out of sight of the window before stepping through the void.

How did you get this number?

I have my sources.

Send me a picture.

Did you lose your mind while I was gone?

Contract

e or Your Company's Name]
ne 1]
ne 2]
Zip Code]

ame or Company's Name]
1]
)
Code]

e or Heading**

Agreement") is made and entered into on [Date], between [Your Name or Company's Name] ("Party A") and or Company's Name] ("Party B").

e or objective of the agreement in clea

ions:**

itions, and re

CHAPTER 7
SLOANE

Seere knowing about the gala where I was being honored was unsettling to say the least. He always knew where I was and with whom. I didn't need a date for the event because I was being presented with an award and didn't have time to find someone to go with me.

It hadn't been easy forming romantic attachments while in Europe for two months—or having a demon at my back.

What I needed more than a date was a massage.

The rest of the day was one client call after another about the supposed "new agent" who was willing to risk it all to steal them away from me. By 6 p.m., I'd only lost one player, and I wasn't too upset that the prima donna had signed a new contract with Ben. It actually meant that I was due a contract avoidance fee. Plus, I no longer had to deal with a right-winger who thought he was the MVP before stepping on the ice.

It was dark by the time I turned onto my street, and I was looking forward to the takeaway I'd ordered being only ten minutes behind me. My most comfortable pajamas were clean and waiting for me on my freshly made bed.

Unfortunately for me and my rousing nighttime plans, there was a massive moving truck parked in front of my driveway.

I honked at one of the men unloading some boxes onto a dolly. He held up both hands as if I were the problem and turned to pick up another box. I put my car in park and got out just in time for another man to emerge from the house with a confused look on his stupid face.

"You parked in front of my garage. I need you to move," I hollered before he got to the end of the driveway.

"Ma'am, I'm so sorry, but we can't move the truck yet. Give us about an hour and we'll be out of your hair—"

"Don't worry about her, Lenny. She can wait for me to unload." Ben's too-familiar smile shifted from kind to cruel when he locked eyes with me. "She always did before."

My fists shook at my sides. I looked from the house that shared a property line with mine then back to Ben.

"What in the fuck are you doing here?"

He hiked a thumb over his shoulder to the men bustling around with moving boxes. "Just getting settled. You wouldn't believe how much stuff can fit in there."

My teeth ground so tight that my jaw ached. "You know what I mean, Ben. Why are you moving into the house right next to mine?"

The mover, who was still lurking, cleared his throat. "I can pull the truck back a bit so she can get to her garage."

Ben didn't break eye contact with me as he answered, "Fine. I'll be a good neighbor and move the truck. Maybe later, you can thank me by treating me to a sweet cream pie."

A shiver of disgust rolled down my spine. Without another word, I returned to my car, slammed the door, and waited for the moving truck to get out of the way.

I seethed until my garage door dropped and I was inside my living room before losing my mind.

I stormed upstairs to my bedroom and into my closet, where I kept my safe. Desperation and fury pulsed through me as I spun the lock. I finally got the damned thing open then took out the small ring Seere had given me years ago. It looked too much like an engagement ring, and for many reasons, I'd hidden it away for times like this.

I slipped the ring on my finger then stomped back down to the living room.

"Seere!"

His name echoed from the tall ceiling. It didn't have a chance to bounce back before I screamed again.

"Seere, I know you can hear me."

"Have you finally decided to confess your deep love and devotion to me?" His voice slithered around me from a dark corner of the living room.

"You promised," I snapped. "You promised that he would never be able to come back and hurt me. You said he would spend the rest of his life miserable and surviving off of the crumbs I permitted him to scavenge. Why is he here, in my city, living in a fucking mansion on my block?"

I was volcanic.

The deal we had struck was worthless if Ben was allowed even a glimpse of happiness.

"Who says he isn't miserable? Have you seen the price of cocaine in this town?" Seere picked at his cuticles, either ignoring me or determined to send me into a rampage.

"If I could, I would kill you right now. You asshole." I moved toward him with my hands miming strangulation.

"You're such a tease." His eyes panned over me, and a masochistic smirk spread over his face. "You know I like it rough."

"What are you going to do about this?" I flung an arm out.

"Nothing." He shrugged.

"Nothing? Nothing?" My anger was unraveling me. "You've broken our agreement. I gave you my soul in exchange for his life in ashes. Yet here he is, unpacking a truck full of crap into the house next to mine."

Seere wagged his finger at me like I was a child having an unwarranted tantrum. "I haven't broken our agreement at all. He lost everything and *is* miserable. But unless you want me to kill him, there's nothing I can do about a rat who found its way to shore from a shipwreck."

"I don't want him dead. I want him to be begging at my feet for forgiveness." I flopped onto the nearest sofa with my face in my hands. "You're pathetic."

"I do wish you'd say that again, but dressed in leather while tightening a vise around my balls."

I looked up at his pleased expression. "You're going to go over there and do something. Keep your real promise to me without any of your fucking demon loopholes."

"I won't be doing that, but what I will do is let you take your anger out on me." He leaned over me and braced his hands on the back of the couch, caging me in. "I love how feisty you get when you're mad. My little flame could burn the world down with that anger."

I huffed. "Useless fucking demon." I got to my feet, pushing him away. "Fine."

He chuckled. "Is this your way of giving me permission to follow you to bed or to kill him?"

I ignored him and marched to my bedroom closet.

Seere appeared in my doorway just in time to watch the largest piece of luggage I owned bounce heavily on my bed. I turned to my dresser, opened the top drawer, and scooped everything out of it. Socks. Panties. Lingerie. Bras. I dumped everything into the suitcase, turned to the next drawer, and repeated the process.

If Seere wasn't going to fix his mistake, I was going to leave the city.

The state.

The country!

Anything to get away from Ben and the demon gawking at me.

"Sloane," he called, but I was already gathering dresses and slacks from my closet. "Sloane. Stop."

"No!" I shouted back at him. "No. I won't. I'm not going to stop until I find some fucking island somewhere you won't be able to find me. Some tiny blip of an island that only fishermen and birds know. If that's what it takes to—"

Seere wrapped his hands around my shoulders and shook me hard enough to stop my rant.

I looked up at his stern expression. Hot tears had welled in my eyes, giving his face a blurred halo and reminding me that at one point, he had been an angel. He must have been so beautiful. Now, he was brutal. He was staring down at me like he was ready to devour me whole. He always gave me that look when I'd pushed him too far and he was ready to remind me that he did, in fact, own me.

"You can start over every single day. Move to a new city. Move to a different country if you like." His face was a breath away from mine. "Distance won't silence the voice in your head that's always searching for me in the dark corners."

A hand smoothed up the nape of my neck while the other slipped to my waist, bringing my hips against his.

"Because I will be in every shadow." The hard length of him pressed to my belly, and the hot surge of danger, fear, and weakness filled my core.

"I can't do this again," I whispered.

"I can." His eyes darkened with the depth of his voice. "I could spend lifetimes chasing you to every hidden pocket of this plane and all others."

The tears I'd been holding back finally broke free,

making trails of my own emotional betrayal obvious. I took a deep breath to chase off the rest.

"He's here," I choked out. "You promised he wouldn't be."

Everything in me was fighting the urge to melt into his hold. It would be too easy to escape into him like I'd done time and time again.

His eyes pinged between mine. "You can't escape the demons you enjoy playing with," he finally said.

Another of his cryptic riddles.

I didn't like feeling cornered by Ben or Seere. At one point, I may have been addicted to the pain of wanting to please men who could never be pleased.

Ben had broken my spirit into pieces he only picked up and looked at when he was bored. I'd praised him for every small favor. My expectations for him as a partner or even a friend were on the floor. Even lower if we were being honest.

Seere was a literal demon who enjoyed the way his former grace had been twisted into the demented power he wielded over all mankind.

For too long, I had pushed away my morality because being with Seere gave me a high that I'd only ever read about in classic love stories. But when his ferociousness showed itself again, the bubble of lust would burst and I would drop into the deepest lows. I could have walked away. But there was something about the way he worshiped me that had me coming back for more.

"You're wrong." I did my best to sound convincing.

"I know you, Sloane. I can feel it in you now. That fire you keep alight just for me."

I pulled out of his arms, and he let me.

I folded my arms over my chest. Looked at him fully. He'd been waiting for me to call. I realized that now. His clothes were fresh, his hair perfectly styled. His cologne was still bright and followed me when I took a step away.

"You say you know me, but you only know my sins."

"I know you better than you think."

"Prove it."

That cocky, crooked smile was back. "You wonder if you've ever truly loved anyone. Men you've dated in the past were either comfortable or obsessions. You've never had a stable relationship that didn't feel boring. Same as you've never been desperate for someone who didn't have their eyes on everything else but you."

The sting of that truth enflamed my cheeks.

I'd only ever loved those who'd hurt or ignored me. I'd only kept men around who were dependable, but I never truly cared if I knew them fully.

The thought had haunted me at night for as long as I could remember.

"You don't know if you're even capable of love." He continued his attack on my already broken heart. "If you dwell on it too long, you don't think you've ever felt or seen pure love."

"Stop, Seere. You've made your point." I needed him to stop before I allowed him to take advantage of the weakness he so clearly saw.

"No, I haven't." His dark tone curled around the stone in my stomach and settled heavily into its new home. "My point won't be made until you admit that you reject me the way you do because you don't want me to get bored. And you don't think you could live with yourself if you let down your guard. Because in the darkest and most depraved recesses of your soul, you're just as obsessed with me as I am with you. And that terrifies you."

"I couldn't love you," I snapped. "You are hate, destruction, and manipulation."

"And what about that is so different than what makes you who you are?"

My eyes widened.

He moved closer. "You summoned me out of hate to destroy a man's life and manipulate his fate."

"He abused me. He hurt me." My voice cracked. "I summoned you to give him a taste of his own medicine."

He nodded but his intense gaze didn't waver as he

edged closer. "For that, I ruined him. And the moment you tire of watching him dangle on the hook, I will rip him apart slowly until nothing but blood and bone are left."

"You enjoy killing and hurting people. That's the difference between us."

"I fell from Grace long ago and have come to peace with my freedom from morality." Finally, his fingers feathered over my bare thigh, my skin coming to life under his touch. "You gave me your soul and nothing will compel me to let you go. When your mortal body leaves this plane, I will follow your soul to the depths of Hell until the end of time. The sooner you accept your unique position, the sooner you can enjoy the aspects of your urges that you suppress because of human expectations."

I wasn't breathing.

"You are tied to an immortal prince. You have no boundaries to abide by. No barriers to climb. Anything on this plane or in Hell is at your disposal so long as you swallow your pride and ask me for it."

My back pressed flat to the wall. His hands clamped under my legs as he forced his body against mine until I was wrapped around his waist. The hem of my skirt rolled up, leaving nothing to cover my lower half but a triangle of lace.

"Each of my brothers can be redeemed. Lust so

easily turns to love. Sloth into self-discovery and well-being. Even envy can be an opportunity for growth. But not me, Sloane. I am violence, rage, and barbaric inhumanity. Every angle of me is sharp, painful, and dangerous. But my broken edges fit yours."

His lips slowly brushed my jaw to my cheekbone. I took a shallow breath, but his hard chest was a rampart, limiting me to small sips of air that only made my head swim even more.

"I hate you."

"Do you remember the last time you said you hated me?" His tongue ran along my bottom lip then flicked the tip of my nose, and a wicked smile completed his lascivious expression.

Of course I remembered. It had been the week before I fled the country and the final nail in the coffin. I'd never been so angry in my life. I'd vowed to never let him affect me like that again.

"The fury in your eyes could have burned empires. The hatred coursed through your veins thicker than your own blood. And all the while, my cock pounded into your pretty little cunt."

My pussy pulsed and my body responded just the way he'd intended as his soft lips took mine. His hips pushed against me, grinding his cock harder over my belly but making me ache to feel him stretch my pussy around him.

"Please," I breathed between slow, agonizing kisses.

His mouth moved down to my chest, trailing from one clavicle to the other.

"Don't." My body clearly didn't get the message my mouth and brain were screaming at it. His hands on my skin burned, and all I wanted was for him to rip every thread off me.

"Use your words, Sloane." He pulled at the top of my blouse then dipped his chin to my hard nipple, hidden in black lace. "What don't you want? For me to stop?"

He flattened his tongue over it, and my back arched to bring him closer. I whispered his name. A final plea for my sanity to return and talk me out of doing something I would regret in the morning.

I heard the zipper of his slacks.

"It's been such a long time. Speak up because I am about to take what I want if you don't."

The head of his cock fought against the fabric of my thong, the last tether keeping us from committing a night full of atrocities.

If I had my way, my heart would have stopped beating out of spite. But instead . . .

"Fuck me."

How did you get this number?

I have my sources.

Send me a picture.

Did you lose your mind while I was gone?

Contract

[Your Name or Your Company's Name]
[Address Line 1]
[Address Line 2]
[City, State, Zip Code]

[Their Name or Company's Name]
[Address]
[City, State, Zip Code]

Title or Heading

This Agreement ("Agreement") is made and entered into on [Date], between [Your Name or Company's Name] ("Party A") and [Their Name or Company's Name] ("Party B").

Purpose or objective of the agreement in clear terms.

Definitions:

Definitions, and responsibilities.

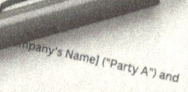

CHAPTER 8
SEERE

I smiled against her neck, the muscles of her throat grazing my teeth as she said what I'd been hoping for all night.

"Fuck me."

A rumble of hunger rose from my chest as I pulled her panties aside. I slipped two fingers into her wet cunt and gave two pumps. Her walls pulsed around me.

I grinned up at her while my thumb teased her clit roughly. "Is this what you wanted?"

"You're such an asshole—oh, fuck." She panted and bucked her hips. "I hate you."

"The way your face lights up when you're furious makes my cock so hard."

Her cheeks reddened, and I circled my digit slower over her swollen nerves. I slipped in a third finger, and her eyelids fluttered. Her inhales partnered with her whines of impatience. Desperate Sloane was my favorite to play with. Any further and she would take control. It was a delicate balance to keep my position.

I pulled my fingers out to their tips then plunged back inside. Curled them to hit the spot that drove her to the edge of an orgasm. Pulled back again.

"Fuck me or get out." She tightened her thighs around me, attempting to lift from my hold.

"You're wearing too many layers to be using such a stern voice." My eyes ate up the sight of her lace bralette.

I flicked my gaze back up to find a challenge there. Did I dare strip her bare and chance her changing her mind, or would she give over all control?

No.

I needed to remind her how it felt to be fucked by the one being who knew her body inside and out.

I lined up the head of my cock to her wet heat and slammed home. The air in my lungs shot from my throat in a grateful moan shaped like her name.

My Sloane.

Mine.

"Oh fuck," she gritted through clenched teeth.

I thrust deeper, pounding her lower back against the wall. "Tell me that you missed this."

Another blow of my hips, chorused by a curse from

her lips. She was close. I could feel it. "Tell me that you're only whole when I'm inside of you."

"No!" she screamed as my pace picked up. "God!"

"He made you for me, Sloane. This pussy was made for me."

She clawed into my shoulder, holding on any way she could.

"That's why it feels so good when I'm inside of you. Why you need me to fuck you like this."

Her head fell to the nape of my neck and her teeth found a spot to tear into. I groaned. My balls tightened, and my lower stomach curled with my mounting orgasm.

"Tell me who owns this pussy, spitfire. Who do you think about when you touch yourself at night?"

She shook her head, holding back the sounds of her pleasure.

"Say it," I grunted.

I wrapped an arm around her back, forcing her clit to grind against me as I delivered round after round of brutal thrusts.

"Come for me, little flame. You're so close."

She refused, biting hard until I could feel my flesh being pierced.

I cursed. Not from pain but from frustration. Her stubbornness and tight pussy were too much.

Pulling out of her completely, I forced her to her

knees. Her eyes tracked up my body slowly, holding all the defiance she let meld with her desire.

"Open." I pumped my cock with my hand.

Her gaze was intent on mine as her lips parted and I forced my way inside. The head of my cock hit the back of her throat. The dark eyeliner around her blue irises started to run from the tears collecting on her lashes.

"You're so fucking beautiful with your mouth full."

I fisted her hair and held her in place, pulsing my hips. Her hands came up to my thighs, but only to dig her nails into the flesh, not stop me from stuffing my cock down her throat again and again until my muscles tensed and I saw stars. The waves of my orgasm rushed from my spine to my limbs as her tongue, jaw, and lips worked me through it.

I braced myself on the wall behind her. She sucked softly until the spasms ceased and every drop was swallowed.

She was the most beautiful woman I'd ever seen, especially when she was on her knees and looking at me like she wanted to stab me with a very dull knife. The frustration on her face brought a smile to mine. I took a handful of her shirt and pulled her to her feet.

"I need to taste us."

I leaned in for a kiss, but she looked away. "You

should go." She pushed past me to walk to the middle of her bedroom.

I pulled my pants up, fastened them, then turned to face her. "Or maybe I should lay you out on that bed and eat your pussy until you forget how much you hate me."

"I don't have eternity." She crossed her arms and refused to look me in the eyes. "I have a long day tomorrow and need to deal with shit on my own. So just. Go."

She was pushing me away like she always did. Her fear cast a pitch-black shadow over what we could have if she would just let me in. I could have killed Ben the moment he'd stepped foot in the States. But I needed her to ask for it.

"Fine." As I walked toward the door I didn't intend to use, I wrapped my arm around her stiff waist and kissed her cheek. I resigned myself once again to her unyielding nature, but not without gaining the last word. "If you run, I'll catch you. If I catch you, then I keep you."

Her eyes locked on mine, and all the fire in Hell couldn't compare to the inferno inside of her.

I returned home slack muscled, but not at all satisfied. More than once while lying in bed and scrolling through social media for hours, I thought about going back to Sloane. She hadn't climaxed on purpose, not giving me the gratification I craved most. Our history was riddled with nights just like this, with her screaming and becoming irate just to have me fuck her aggravation away.

Though I wasn't as delusional as some of my other brothers, I did believe Sloane's body had been made for me. Not by our Father specifically, that was too close for comfort, but it was rare to find a human body that could handle my hunger.

In fact, she often begged for more. More marks from my teeth or palm. Rougher sex that made it hard for her to walk straight the next day. When we were together, there were very few hard limits. She'd done things to my body that no one else would be permitted to do and enjoyed the power she had over me.

Those nights had followed me when I'd pursued her through Europe. Chasing her had been an easy choice. Restraining myself when she pushed me away like she had tonight was infuriating. She was denying me the pleasure of seeing her back arch and her face contort as the orgasm gripped her and pulled her under.

If this was another point of attack to bore me, she'd

done the opposite. Running from me only drew me further in. I was hungry for her more than ever. The need to feel my teeth scrape over the soft flesh of her neck, breasts, and thighs fueled my obsession. I needed to hear the sound of my hand snapping her ass as my hips clapped furiously against her backside.

My spine tingled at the image of her on her knees before me. The soulless being that existed only for chaos, pain, and vengeance battled with the urge to do unspeakable things to her. That bastard part of me wanted to own Sloane and use her until her screams of pleasure turned into cries of pain.

She'd tamed that beast the first time my true name had passed through her lips. A soft gasp and a wanton moan were all it had taken to soothe the gnawing need for fresh blood on my hands. Yet here I was with only memories of her body.

I scrolled through our short text thread. It wasn't enough to scratch the itch of needing her.

SEERE

Are you done pouting?

My bubble indicated that she'd read the message. I waited for a reply but several minutes passed without one.

SEERE

I guess not.

> Fine.
>
> I'll just have to show up at your office tomorrow and fuck that attitude out of you in front of your assistant.

SLOANE

> Don't you dare.

SEERE

> Why not?
>
> Don't you remember the first time I visited you at work?

SLOANE

> I had to lay off that assistant with a full year of severance to bribe him to delete the photos he took.

SEERE

> Should have told me. I would have taken care of it.

SLOANE

> I didn't need you to take care of it.
>
> I need you to stop fucking me in public.

SEERE

> That's reasonable.
>
> I promise to only fuck you in the privacy of my own home.
>
> Come over.

SLOANE

You were literally just here.

SEERE

I was.

Come over.

SLOANE

No.

SEERE

Your pussy misses me.

She didn't get filled with my cum like she likes.

SLOANE

Stop talking about my vagina like it's a person.

We just had sex. You got off and I feel stupid for letting it happen.

SEERE

Demanded.

SLOANE

Excuse me?

SEERE

You demanded that I fuck you.

You're not stupid. You're stubborn.

SLOANE

Thanks for that clarification.

SEERE

You're right though.

I did get off.

Come over and so will you.

SLOANE

I'm good.

SEERE

Did you think of me while you were touching yourself?

SLOANE

No. I wanted to come, not vomit.

SEERE

You have such a sassy mouth when you don't get yours.

Come over and I'll make it up to you.

SLOANE

I said I'm good.

SEERE

All right, new offer then.

Come over and let me get my fill of you.

SLOANE

Why would I do that?

SEERE

Because making you come on my face for hours would be great for your complexion.

SLOANE

Worried about my skincare now?

SEERE

Extremely.

You looked run-down. Tired.

A few dozen orgasms will make your cheeks glow.

SLOANE

Insulting me to get me into bed?

That is new.

SEERE

Come over and I'll apologize.

SLOANE

Good night, Seere.

I tapped out a message then deleted it. She was still speaking to me, but if I pushed too hard, she wouldn't. Whatever reasons she'd had to point me to the door earlier tonight weren't enough for her to ignore a late-night text.

The most effective message had been sent. She would be thinking about me until she fell asleep. For tonight, that would be my biggest win.

How did you get this number?

I have my sources.

Send me a picture.

Did you lose your mind while I was gone?

Contract

[Name or Your Company's Name]
[Line 1]
[Line 2]
[Zip Code]

[Name or Company's Name]
[1]
[2]
[Code]

Title or Heading

This Agreement ("Agreement") is made and entered into on [Date], between [Your Name or Company's Name] ("Party A") and [Name or Company's Name] ("Party B").

Purpose or objective of the agreement in clear terms.

Conditions:

...litions, and...

CHAPTER 9
SLOANE

Seere hadn't changed. I hadn't expected him to, but what he'd said before he fucked me was all too true.

I couldn't live with myself if I finally gave in to him and he grew bored of me.

I'd cried myself to sleep for many reasons, but that was one that haunted me the most.

After I'd dropped out of school at Ben's request, my family stopped speaking to me. Even after I'd laid the groundwork for my company and had started to make a hefty salary, my parents had rarely contacted me. I wasn't the daughter they'd raised. My mother told me too often that she hardly recognized the person I had become.

Knowing that I'd disgraced my family name had made it that much easier to stay in the States, gain citizenship, and open one of the most successful sports agencies run by women. Not that the pot was all that wide to start. But every one of my employees was paid fairly and well taken care of. My boys—the sluts that they were—all respected me and knew I would fight harder for them than any of my male colleagues.

Seere always managed to see past all my good and delve into my darkest, most insecure places to weaken me. Perhaps he was trying to bring light to my vulnerability in order to force me to be empowered by it. I didn't need him to act like a spiritual counselor. I didn't need him at all, in fact. At least that was what I told myself so I could slip into sleep, only to dream about him plowing me into my mattress.

The next morning, I went to the gym to release my frustration and pent-up emotional trauma. It was early still. The fog had rolled in from the ocean, clinging to windows of cars and clouding the streetlights in the parking lot.

Often, my exercise routine included group classes, but I needed to run until I could sweat out the toxins I'd swallowed the night before. I locked my purse up then found my favorite treadmill. It was far enough from the door that I wouldn't feel the draft every time it opened, and it was in the second row, which meant it was less likely to fill up than the first.

With my headphones firmly in place, I started the machine and my running playlist, which was mostly nineties boy bands, some nostalgic pop-country, and the latest songs that had made their way from social media to mainstream popularity. It only took a few minutes for the world to fall away and for the serenity of anonymity to take over. I wasn't a powerful NHL agent or someone's ex-girlfriend, and certainly not the object of a demon's twisted obsession. I was just running.

Twenty minutes into my cathartic cardio session, a large someone stepped onto the treadmill next to mine. I looked down the row to see only two other machines were in use. Assuming the newcomer was a creep who didn't understand personal boundaries or gym etiquette, I turned the music up in my headphones and tried my best to block out his presence.

Until there was a tap on my shoulder.

It was Ben. At my fucking gym.

I balanced my feet on either side of the treadmill frame then took off my headphones. "Why in the fuck are you here?"

My lungs squeezed. Each of my labored breaths was tight, and if I wasn't already red from running, my cheeks would be on fire for a different reason.

"I heard this was the best gym around. Thought I'd stop by and be neighborly." He shrugged his giant muscular shoulders then leaned over the rail of his machine. "Hey, neighbor."

He was hardly dressed for a workout. His T-shirt was crisp and looked like it had never seen a bead of sweat. His sweatpants looked like they were for fashion, not lifting weights. And if his outfit weren't a dead giveaway that he'd only come to harass me, his hair looked like he'd just finished primping and teasing it.

"Whatever you're trying to do, you're out of your league." I wiped the sweat from my brow with the back of my hand.

"I own this league, sweetheart. Remember?"

I wanted to slap the sadistic smile right off his face. Instead of committing a violent act that would get me banned from my gym, I stopped the machine, grabbed my keys and water bottle, and made a quick getaway to the locker room.

"You look good, by the way," he called after me. "Bad-ass sports agent life really suits you. Too bad you didn't have this sort of dedication when we were together."

I locked myself in one of the shower stalls in the ladies' room and took my time washing, conditioning, and drying my hair. I figured he would get bored and leave by the time I grabbed everything from my locker.

Had he stalked me? How else could he have known where I lived or worked out?

I pushed it out of my head. It would only rattle me further, and I had to keep my wits about me if I was going to outsmart him in whatever game he was playing.

I slammed the locker door shut and took my phone out of my bag. The screen lit up in my hand to show three missed text notifications.

SEERE

Are you wearing black or red tonight?

I'd prefer you wear red.

You look ravishing in red.

SLOANE

Don't worry about what I'm wearing. You're not going.

The last thing I needed was Seere showing up anywhere I was.

Another text came in from Seere, but I ignored it. Whatever smart-ass remark he had could wait until I got to the office. I hauled my gym tote onto my shoulder and headed to the door. To my misfortune, standing just outside the ladies' locker room was Ben. I rolled my eyes and continued to the main exit, ignoring him, but he jogged up to me before I made it outside.

"Leaving so soon?" He folded his arms across his

chest, enforcing the wall he'd become between me and sanity.

"Yes." I stepped to the side, and he followed.

"Heard you had quite the day at work yesterday, seeing as I went after all your boys. I needed to get your attention, and by the way you're behaving, I did."

"I hope Charles works out for you instead of spending his first quarter in the sheets and giving nothing to the game. A real winner you got there."

"He won't be the last."

"What?"

"You heard me." He sized me up like we were about to go ten rounds hand to hand. "I'm coming for you, babe."

"You've lost your mind." I stepped around him, and this time he didn't follow.

Instead, he waited until I was in my car and came up to the window to knock. I shook my head, but he knocked again.

"Just leave, Sloane," I whispered to myself, taking a deep breath. "Start your car and leave. You don't owe him any of your attention."

"Want to come to a truce?" His muffled voice came through the window. "Dinner. That's all I want. I'm even willing to make a trade for Johana."

Shit.

Jasper Johana was a newer player but showed

potential for greatness. I felt it in my bones. He wouldn't just win tourneys. He was destined for the Hall Of Fame. I cracked the window. "For who?" I knew it was a trap, but if I was careful, it would work out in my favor.

He took a half step back, waiting for me to roll the window down more, but I refused. If he was going to act like a pathetic dog, he could bark at me through a sheet of glass.

"We'll see," he said proudly.

I thought about it for a moment. More than the player he was offering—one I'd been drooling over for months since his last contract had lapsed with an agent who didn't do him justice—I wanted more than anything to humiliate Ben. Trading a weaker player for a top-ranking center who had the potential to win a career full of tournaments would be a career-ending move for Ben.

"Lunch. Not dinner," I countered.

"Deal."

I took one of my cards from the dashboard compartment and slipped it through the sliver of open window.

He took it and put it into his pocket. "I'll call you later."

"Email only."

His brow rose, but he didn't argue.

With that, he walked away. Not back to the gym, but to his Lexus.

Fucking asshole.

My phone vibrated in my lap.

SEERE
> I made myself clear last night.
>
> Black or red?

SLOANE
> You're not invited.

SEERE
> How about you wear a black dress but red panties?
>
> I can compromise.
>
> It won't matter. I'll be ripping it all off of you by the end of the night.

I didn't answer, but the image of that scenario followed me all the way to work.

How did you get this number?

I have my sources.

Send me a picture.

Did you lose your mind while I was gone?

Contract

[Name or Your Company's Name]
[Line 1]
[Line 2]
[, Zip Code]

[Name or Company's Name]
[1]
[2]
[Code]

tle or Heading

"Agreement") is made and entered into on [Date], between [Your Nam... mpany's Name] ("Party A") and
 or Company's Name] ("Party B").

e or objective of the agreement in clea...

tions:**

ditions, and re... erms.

CHAPTER 10
SEERE

I watched from the front seat of my car as Sloane drove off from the gym. She'd given Ben her card, and all the wheels of that action spun in my head. She either wanted to lure him into some plan she'd come up with on her own or was genuinely curious about whatever he'd proposed to her. And he had asked her for something. Her lips formed the answer twice before he'd followed her out to her car.

My palms itched to make that man bleed for even looking at my spitfire. Depending on what information I found today while tailing him, he would be a bruised and battered pile by the end of the week.

Ben started to drive out of the parking lot. I gave him a head start and kept three car lengths between us until he pulled into the garage of a dingy-looking building on a sketchy road in the heart of the city. I kept to the shadows while I followed him into an underground elevator. This was where a very special skill came in handy. I let the light and shadows refract against my whole being, making me essentially invisible.

I slipped into the lift with him right before he punched the button to the top floor. He pulled his phone from his pocket along with the card Sloane had given him. His thumbs tapped out a message as he bit his lip like a smitten frat boy.

He wasn't much better than some keg-chasing college asshole. He'd played professional hockey for years and had squeezed every advantage out of it. He'd slept with anything that moved, no matter that Sloane had been waiting at home for him for most of those years. Coaching or becoming an agent himself were the only paths left after his injury—by my hands, mind you.

Even now, his hip was cocked to alleviate the weight on the knee that he'd had replaced. I hadn't stopped with his legs. His shoulder had suffered a horrifically painful tear that had taken months of rehab to repair. Three of his teeth were false. And when he breathed too deeply, the old cracked ribs he'd obtained still bothered him.

He was a mess. But he was still alive.

My mistake. I shouldn't have allowed such a thing.

Sloane had wanted him to watch her succeed. She had wanted to be able to keep tabs on how far he'd fallen because of her.

Perhaps it was my fault that Ben had found a way to sneak up on us. She had been too preoccupied fleeing from me to see the snake in the grass. The deal she and I had struck kept me from killing him as much as it kept her soul bound to me. There were no loopholes like she'd accused me of.

"I want him to suffer for the rest of my life." That was what she'd said. Which meant that as long as her body still held signs of life, so would his.

The elevator finally came to a stop, and Ben sauntered into a large open room where several lesser demons were working. I recognized them in an instant. They were marked with my brother Gaap's sigil. The Prince of Sloth had been absent from his throne for decades. His legion of lesser spirits should have been delighted to serve my other princely brothers, but it was clear these demons had no leadership.

A tall, thin demon wearing all black broke away from the rest and met Ben in the middle of the floor.

"What are you doing here?" the lowly demon snarled, but Ben didn't cower.

"I wanted to be sure our deal was actually going to go into effect," Ben answered, holding up his phone to show the demon something. "Sloane's business hasn't been affected at all. Only one of her clients turned on her, and he was basically useless."

"I told you, the magic surrounding her is more powerful than mine. Whoever she made a deal with ensured she was protected, not just marked. You're going to have to do your own legwork to tear her life apart."

My fingernails dug into my palms. How dare they defy the orders of the princes of Hell.

My magic was distinct. This demon knew who he was fucking with. There was no denying to whom Sloane's soul was tethered.

"She didn't bargain for her career," Ben shot back. "Why hasn't it crumbled like the others I've fucked with?"

The lesser spirit shrugged. His patience was gone for the human who'd made a loose deal with him. "You'll have to figure it out. Now get out before you attract the wrong kind of attention."

Ben turned away with a huff and got back into the elevator.

I followed until I was standing at the threshold. As the doors started to close, I unveiled myself. Ben's eyes bulged at the wicked, vicious smile spread across my face. He cursed as I let the doors close. Then I turned around to find a room full of lesser demon scavengers staring at me with all the surprise of children caught with their hands in the cookie jar.

"Well, look what we have here," I said into the room.

The silence was broken by someone saying, "Oh fuck."

Then the screaming began.

COVERED IN INKY-BLACK DEMON BLOOD, I stepped into The Red Room. Semper, the demonic manager, came out of the office to greet me.

"Ruby called in sick. Journey and Margot will have to go on first. Whoa . . . what happened to you? Are you hurt?" Her mouth hung open while her eyes searched for the source of blood I was covered in.

"I had to remind a few lesser spirits of their place."

"By killing them?"

I shrugged. "They fucked with Sloane." I grabbed a towel from the bar back and smeared the tar-like residue from my face.

"Oh, well, in that case." Her eyes widened in a mock show of agreement and she went back to the mental checklist she had been rattling off. "Beatrice will be late but will be here by her second set. I can move Clementine to fill the void."

"That is what Clem does best." I gave her a cheeky wink, and she shook her head.

"And that is all I have for the day." She pulled off the sweatshirt she was wearing to reveal her dancing clothes. "What sort of trouble have you been up to?"

"Nothing out of the ordinary. But it looks like I'll have to clean up the mess that was made by one of my brothers who should have been more concerned about his duties than fucking holes in every country."

"Who's fucking holes?" One of the dancers came striding out on the stage in nothing but her shoes.

"Lexx, you need to at least be in a thong," Semper scolded with a pointed finger to the back of the stage. "You know the rules. This isn't Vegas."

Lexx was one of our bisexual dancers who drew in the few straight men who tended to tag along with their lesbian friends. She was tall, thin, blonde, and overly augmented. Her breasts and ass were fully rounded while the rest of her didn't hold an ounce of fat.

Her lips made a deliberate pout as she crouched down and spread her knees wide. She bounced on the balls of her feet and watched for any sort of reaction from me. It wouldn't come. Though she did stir a new fantasy of Sloane spreading herself for me center stage while a crowd watched me devour her.

When I raised a brow of confusion, Lexx closed her legs. In a smooth motion, her hips shifted from one side to the other to stand. The disappointment and challenge in her eyes were a dangerous combination, I knew. It wouldn't be the first time jealousy and wrath had mixed into a volatile cocktail against me. But Lexx and my issues with Gaap would have to wait.

I pulled out my phone and called Sloane.

"What?" she answered.

I couldn't help but smile. "Come see me."

"Are you seriously booty-calling me? It's not even 10 a.m."

"Depends on if you're offering to trade information for a taste of your—"

"That's enough. Information about Ben?"

"Come see me and I'll tell you." I shot a glance at Semper, who was shaking her head at the foolish smile on my face.

"If this is a trick, I swear to God, Seere, I will run you through with a rusty kitchen knife."

"Promises, promises. You never follow through with the acts of passion you threaten."

"Only you would think violence is sexual."

I would let this woman hold a dagger to my balls while she rode me if that was what she needed to get off. There was a rustling behind her voice that shook me from the vision of Sloane's supple tits bouncing in my face.

"Are you leaving your office? It sounds like you're leaving your office."

She sighed. "Yes, I'm leaving my office. I'll be there in half an hour."

"How many weapons are you bringing?"

"Seere." Her tone carried a warning. "I'm not kidding. I will rip your balls off if you're lying to get me in your sleazy club."

The sound of her car starting came through.

I sucked in a breath through my teeth. "Slow down, little flame. I'm already close to coming from all this dirty talk."

Her line went dead, and I locked my screen with a low chuckle. I looked up to see Semper watching me with her hands on her cocked hips.

"What?" I put my hands up innocently.

"You're a dog." She shook her head and turned to walk to the back office. "Don't fuck on the bar. I just sanitized it."

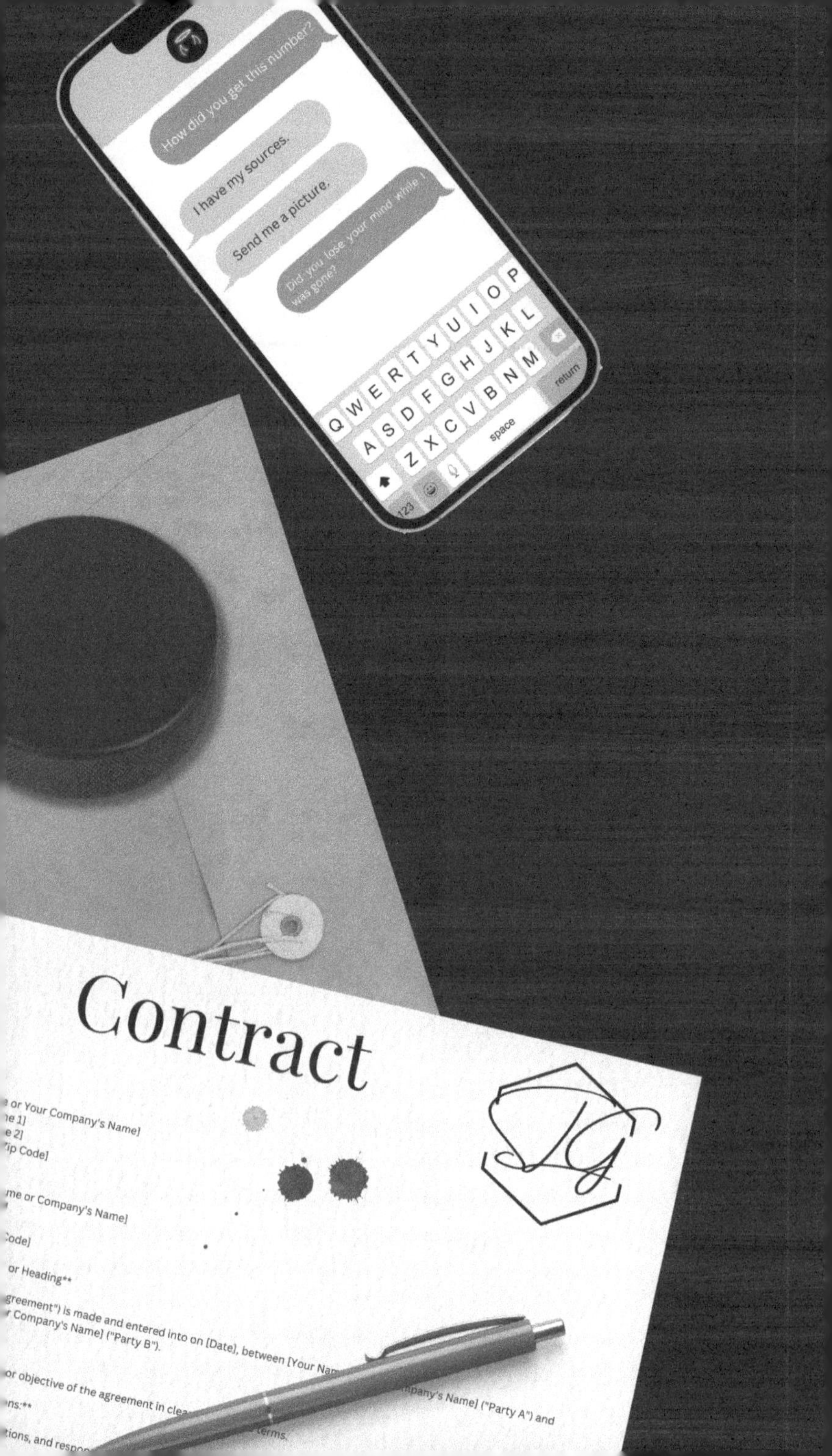
How did you get this number?
I have my sources.
Send me a picture.
Did you lose your mind while I was gone?
Contract

CHAPTER 11
SLOANE

I hauled open the door to the club and walked onto the main floor. Several dancers were on the stage, practicing. The client seats were empty, but it was getting close to noon so they would be filing in soon.

Seere stood on a small stepladder behind the bar, restocking the liquor. A woman wearing nothing but a thong stood beside him, handing him bottle after bottle of booze. When she heard the door close, she peeked over her shoulder then smiled up at Seere.

She was gorgeous. I supposed I shouldn't be surprised, but something about seeing her next to Seere and enjoying being close to him sent a streak of jealousy through me. But I was the one he was obsessed with. I was the only person he was chasing. That thought lifted my chin as I approached.

When I got a few feet from them, I cleared my throat.

The woman turned and leaned her perky breasts over the dark wood. "What can I do for you, beautiful?"

I pointed my chin at Seere. "I'm here for him."

Her pink tongue grazed over her glossy brown lips. Butterflies stirred low in my belly. "Pity." Her dark eyes took me in from the tips of my shoes to the top of my head. "We could have had a lot of fun together."

"You're pushing your luck, Semper," he said without turning.

The woman snickered, and I smiled, knowing exactly what to say to get under his skin.

"Are you free later?" I asked.

Seere turned immediately and gave Semper a single command. "Out." He pointed toward the stage then hopped to the ground next to her. He was over a foot taller, but she didn't give any sign of being intimidated by the prince of Hell.

Semper chuckled before she blew me a kiss then joined the rest of the dancers, who were watching us. One of them eyed me longer than the rest. She looked from me to Seere several times before one of the other dancers called her attention away.

When I slung my gaze back to Seere, he'd spread

his hands out on the bar to brace himself. His hungry eyes followed me while I took the seat across from him.

"You have a lot of beautiful women here." I threw a glance back over to the stage.

"I only see one."

The connotation of that statement liquified my insides. I crossed my legs, trying to dull the ache between them. The husky tone of his voice reminded me of everything he'd said when he was fucking me last night. How I had been made for him. In his world, that was probably true. My human body had been made to be his, and he was the only man who made me feel . . . anything.

Even the way he was standing before me was possessive. He could have turned the two feet of thick bartop between us into splinters if he decided it was too much distance. Or it could become the next surface where he took what he needed from me. Because, as he reminded me often, he *needed* me.

"What did you find out about Ben?" I did my best to sound like I wasn't reliving the moments when I'd been on my knees before him.

His lips twisted into that crooked smile. "He's working with demons."

Lust turned to ash on my tongue. "He's what?"

"I've slaughtered the source." He was a serial killer who appreciated his work far too much.

"So, you fixed the problem?"

"Possibly." His shoulders rose then fell in a flippant shrug. "To be safe, I should sleep between your legs until we know the outcome."

"Not a chance." I smirked.

"All right, but you're taking an awfully big risk sleeping alone." He leaned forward on his forearms and grinned at me.

"The solution to one monster is not another in my bed."

He raked a hand through his hair, letting the dark strands fall over his face in a curtain that only made his blue eyes shine brighter. His roguish smile made something clamp around my lungs and squeeze. The way he made my insides both melt and freeze up was a magic all its own. Even when I was at my wit's end with him, he had a way of pulling the right strings to make me smile.

"What about my bed, then? He won't find you there."

I narrowed my eyes. "I'm not falling for that again."

"Are you sure?"

Memories of spending three days locked away in his bedroom while I missed client calls, emails, and all other responsibilities surfaced. We hardly slept or ate. What had felt like hours had actually been days of delusional, intense sex.

"Seere." I gave him a warning that he was starting to push too far. In reality, we both knew that I was only trying to convince myself.

"We'll talk about it tonight."

"No. We won't."

"Oh right. You have plans." He ran his knuckle over my clasped hands, a soft and delicate touch that held too many meanings.

"Yes, I do." I pulled my hands into my lap.

"You'll call me when you get bored of all those stuffy intellectuals?" One of his brows rose in expectation.

"You have several doctoral degrees in six countries and have read thousands of books."

He stood up straight, looking as if I'd slandered him. "I am a despicable Hell monster." He panned his hand down his body then waved his arm over his head "I own a strip club."

"And you speak every dead language there's ever been. No matter how L.A. grunge you try to appear, you will always be the most intellectual in every room. Which makes you the boring one by your own standards."

"Fair point, but I fuck better than any other." He winked.

"I wouldn't know." I got to my feet. "But I'll fuck a few tonight and let you know how they compare."

He laughed and shook his head. "Provoking me won't end well for you, spitfire."

I turned to walk toward the door. "It never does."

"You won't be saying that later," he yelled after me.

"Don't call me anymore."

Ben emailed me twice, but I refused to read them until tomorrow.

Tonight, I was getting ready for a gala to commemorate my acts in the community and was being presented by Maxine, my best friend and the one person on this planet who had helped me when I decided to build my firm. She was a corporate lawyer and, ironically enough, worked with someone I shouldn't know about.

Not a prince of Hell, but a duke.

Zepar was cutthroat in the boardroom. It had taken me three encounters with him before I realized why his boldness was so familiar. The way he owned every room he walked into and didn't leave until he got what he wanted reminded me of Seere. And, no surprise, he'd sensed the mark Seere had put on my soul. Needless to say, we'd hit it off.

Zepar and his wife, Mara, were both gorgeous, but their mutual obsession with each other was swoon worthy. Zepar only had eyes for Mara, and that sort of power drew people to her. She had learned a lot from her partner, but she also had a kind nature that you inherently wanted to shield from the wolves in the room.

When I arrived at the hotel ballroom where the gala was being held, Mara was the first to greet me.

"Sloane, you look so hot." She held out her arms, taking me in with her eyes before embracing me.

"So do you, honey. Those gems are to die for." I pulled back and admired the carats of diamonds and rubies lining her neck.

"Thanks, babe. I'm glad you're here. I won't be bored out of my mind all night." She scrunched her nose and looked around at what felt like a sea of humans.

"You're bored of me already?" Zepar's silky voice came over her shoulder as he wrapped his arms around her middle.

"Never." She smiled up at him. "But you've already told me that I couldn't whisk you away to some linen closet somewhere for a quickie, so I'm glad to have a friend here."

A friend.

Hard to believe a demon considered me her friend.

Or that demons could form connections like that. But that was unfair. I only knew a few, and the one I knew intimately was Hell walking.

"I have to go chat up the CEO of Solar Star. His daughter is of interest to one of our princes. Time to welcome her into the fold." Zepar's cocky grin sent a flutter to my stomach.

He was in his element, and not being on the receiving end of a demonic foxhunt made it easy for me to appreciate the artistry. He and Mara waved and disappeared into the crowd.

Maxine knew how to put together a party of influential people. Deals and careers were made at parties like this. CEOs, top lawyers, and politicians all mingled in the dimly lit ballroom.

One thing that Maxine excelled at was ambiance. She could take the coldest event space and turn it into a candlelit affair that felt inviting, cozy, and, best of all, a little sensual. When men felt like they were being romanced and seduced, they were eager to open their wallets. But that wasn't my focus tonight. I had a full billing of clients, even with one less ass on pine.

The festivities would start any minute, and I was getting nervous.

I looked around at the faceless people roaming around, unsure about where I was supposed to be.

Taking my phone out of my clutch, I was planning to call Maxine for directions when a pair of eyes caught my attention.

Staring back at me was Seere's intense gaze. The wolfish grin on his face showed how proud he was that some sort of bat signal had brought my consciousness to him.

Cursing under my breath, I turned and walked toward the stage on the opposite side of the room. It was the place Maxine would most likely be, and I needed to regretfully excuse myself from the event. She would be disappointed, but it would be better than my career ending because a demon with no self-control was lurking in the audience.

I hadn't expected Seere to show and that was my own bêtise.

Whether he actually materialized or he was just that quick to catch up to me, I didn't know, but I blinked and ran into the solid mass of his chest. "Hello, little flame. You look tantalizing this evening."

He backed me into a corner. We were nearly invisible in the dark shadow of a large planter and gauzy drapes.

Seere stared at me through thick lashes, and my lungs struggled for air.

"Weren't you expecting me?" His question was

more sneering than inquisitive. "I should be a part of all major events in your life, don't you think?"

"I thought you got the hint that I didn't want you here." I looked over his shoulder. The people around us were unaware of the monster that was no longer stalking its prey; it had been snared.

His knuckle hooked under my chin and brought my eyes back to his.

"What hint was that? I must have misheard you while you had my cock in your mouth last night."

My cheeks flamed. The shame and guilt twisted around my stomach.

His fingers played at the hem of my short dress. "Where's your date? I'd love to meet him. Show him all the places that make you scream."

The hot tips of his fingers grazed my inner thighs and drew up to the front of my panties.

I clenched, but it was already obvious that my body had betrayed me from the moment the dark, woody scent of his cologne surrounded me. A flashback to our encounter last night freshened the memory of the taste of him and awakened an ache in my core.

Fuck. I hated how easily his touch sent me to the edge.

I gripped his wrist, halting his hand from dipping into the lace. "Someone is going to see you and my reputation will be a disaster."

"Is that what you're so worried about? Someone seeing the filthy girl you really are for me?"

"Everyone can see you." I didn't know if that was true. I didn't dare tear my gaze away from his.

"They'll watch like hyenas as I fuck you against this wall. What a show your screams of pleasure would be."

"Seere," I breathed, my dress tightening around my chest. "Please."

"Mmm, I love it when you whisper my name like you could fall apart if I touch the right spot." Light glinted off his carnivorous grin.

"Not here."

He pulled my hand away and forced his knee between mine. The pads of two of his fingers circled my clit, and his hot breath hit my ear.

"Then where, Sloane? You've edged me at every corner of this earth for too long. I'm positively starved for your undivided attention. And what better place to do that than at a celebration in your honor?"

His free hand swept up the inside of my arm to the column of my throat. The threat of being taken in front of everyone, knowing that this demon could not wait to get me alone so he could touch me, both terrified me and sent heat to my core.

"Shh." I felt his lips curl into a satisfied, triumphant smirk. "Don't move. You're almost there, aren't you?"

My breath hitched as he plunged two fingers inside of me.

"Sloane?"

My eyes flew open and locked on Maxine's.

Contract

[Text visible on phone screen:]
- How did you get this number?
- I have my sources.
- Send me a picture.
- Did you lose your mind while I was gone?

[Contract fragments visible:]

e or Your Company's Name]
ne 1]
ne 2]
Zip Code]

ame or Company's Name]
]

Code]

e or Heading**

greement") is made and entered into on [Date], between [Your Na... or Company's Name] ("Party B").

or objective of the agreement in clea... ...pany's Name] ("Party A") and

ons:**

tions, and... ...terms.

CHAPTER 12
SEERE

"Umm. It's time for the award announcement, but if you're busy . . ."

The human who interrupted us gawked, but I couldn't blame her. Sloane was melting in my hand. She looked so fucking perfect when she was gasping.

"Tell her to leave before I make you come while she watches." I inched my fingers deeper.

Sloane's fingernails sank into my arm, but I didn't move.

"No," Sloane squeaked to her friend. "I'm ready. I'm right behind you, Maxie." Then she lowered her voice for only me. "I promise, if you stop right now and don't make a scene in front of one of the only true friends I have, we'll talk later."

The pressure from the heel of my palm made her clit pulse.

I lowered my lips to the shell of her ear and felt the shiver of her body against mine. "I don't want to talk. I want to hear your greedy moans while you ride my face."

Thrust.

"Talking won't satisfy the hunger I have for just." Thrust. "One." Thrust. "Taste."

"Seere, please. Oh fuck, you're going to make me—"

I ripped my hand away from her throat and covered her mouth. "That's right, spitfire. Come for me. Only me."

My cock strained in my slacks, and I had half a mind to take Sloane through the void and fuck her properly. But her knees buckled, and the noise from the ballroom around us came rushing back. I withdrew my fingers and pulled her dress back down.

A quick glance behind me confirmed that Maxine hadn't witnessed Sloane coming apart for me, and neither had anyone else.

I looked back at Sloane and found her heavy gaze locked on mine. I brought my dripping fingers up to my lips and sucked them clean while she watched.

"Fucking delicious." I stuck my tongue out and teased the seam of her lips.

Sloane's eyes closed. Her mouth opened to let me in. My cock throbbed as she sucked her essence off my taste buds. I groaned and rolled my hips on her belly.

When she looked at me like that, I was helpless. She could command me to burn this plane to the ground and I would burst into flame. I would bring her the wings of every single angel that still resided in Heaven. Anything she wished for I would give her—except for the one thing she insisted she wanted.

"You have to let go of me." She'd caught her breath.

"I don't. But I will."

I pulled away gently, allowing her to regain her balance before I straightened my jacket and turned toward the crowd while she regained her composure.

Maxine was on the stage, reading the list of Sloane's honors and achievements. The crowd clapped during each deliberate pause.

"Congratulations on the award, you earned it," I said over my shoulder. "We'll have a real celebration later."

Sloane didn't say a word as she walked past me and into the light. I watched her make her way to the stage but stepped through the void and into The Red Room before her name was announced.

My cock was rock hard and my balls were painful when I stepped out of the void and into my office. I'd wanted to show Sloane that I could be there for her when she needed support, but my lust got the better of me. How could it not when she eye-fucked me subconsciously every time we were in the same room.

I pulled at my belt that was cutting into my hips and fell back into the chair behind my desk. Dancing was in full swing, and the music from Semper and Clementine's set on the main stage was pounding against the tinted window.

Their legs were up in the air as their torsos swung around their poles in a display of athletic prowess. Rows of women and a smattering of men hollered from their seats and threw cash onto the stage. One of the other dancers was prowling around the crowd, collecting bills in her G-string. When her face turned up, I realized it was Lexx. I didn't usually keep close tabs on everyone's schedules, but since I'd seen her earlier in the day, I didn't expect her to still be here.

She made a beeline for my office, and I straightened when she walked in, closed the door, then sat at the edge of my desk.

"What's up, Lexx?" I said, clasping my hands in my lap.

"You looked lonely." Her breathy voice sounded childlike. "Thought you'd like some company."

Her ass scooted across the dark wood until she was almost in my lap. She lifted her leg and swung it over my head, straddling the space I'd put between us by leaning back.

"Or maybe you're bored and just want a good show?" She arched her back and smoothed two fingers between her breasts, over her stomach, and down to her crotch.

I jumped to my feet. "For fuck's sake, Lexx."

She gripped my shirt and pulled me into her. I slammed my hands onto the desk on either side of her, catching myself. She lay back and ground her hips over my now-flaccid cock, trying to rouse it to life.

Before Sloane, I would have taken an attempt like this as a moment of rebellion to be punished. But now, Sloane was the only being I would have flipped onto her stomach, spanked, then plowed until she was raw.

"I want to make you feel good, my prince. You're always so tense from chasing that little human around." Her hooded eyes landed on my zipper. "I wouldn't run from the wild and violent animal lurking under the surface. Let him free on me."

With a firm hand, I gripped her face and leaned down until we were mere inches away.

"That little human is the only thing keeping me whole. The wild beast you want to bring out of me would tear you to shreds for even implying Sloane isn't worth my time."

Her eyes bulged. "I'm sorry."

I let her go, walked to the door, then opened it. "You're one of our best employees, Lexx, but if you ever try to seduce me or speak about Sloane like that again, I will enact my status and send you back to Hell for all eternity."

She got to her feet and flipped her hair before sashaying past me and back into the club.

I watched from the window as she rejoined the clients. Semper stole a glance at me, and I gave her a reassuring nod. This was Lexx's only warning. Because if I were being more truthful, I would rather have Semper handle it than send Lexx back to Hell. Though Lexx would probably prefer the latter.

After another hour or so, I planned to go home. It wasn't where I wanted to be, but Sloane would call sooner or later. I'd left her only partially satisfied in the hope that she would be ready for another sparring match.

Contract

ne or Your Company's Name]
ine 1]
ine 2]
Zip Code]

Name or Company's Name]
1]
2]
Code]

le or Heading**

"Agreement") is made and entered into on [Date], between [Your Na
or Company's Name] ("Party B").

se or objective of the agreement in clea   pany's Name] ("Party A") and

tions:**

ditions, and res

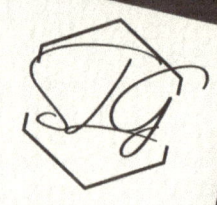

CHAPTER 13
SLOANE

Seere was nowhere in the crowd while I accepted my award. I'd walked onto the stage with my thighs slick with the proof of my shame. When Maxine asked who my mysterious stranger was, the lies I would normally tell wouldn't come.

"He's just some guy I hate," I had said, face red.

"Hate? It didn't seem that way to me."

"Yeah, well. Things aren't always what they seem."

Hours of chatting with guests, fellow lawyers, players I had signed, and too many other faces I didn't have names for fell away and I was on my way home when I started wondering why Seere had shown up. There had to be a reason that had nothing to do with his fingers invading me in public.

I'd have to wait to find out what that reason was

because there was a large figure standing in my driveway when I pulled in.

Ben.

I hadn't emailed him back about lunch but didn't think it was urgent enough that he would show up in front of my house.

"What do you want?" I slammed the car door and didn't wait for him to speak before I started walking to the front step of my house.

"I thought you would email me back by now. Too busy fucking some investment banker?"

"What?" I dug through my purse for my keys.

I hadn't expected to need them so quickly since I usually entered my house through my garage.

"You look like you're coming back from a date, and judging by the outfit and time of night, I'm assuming he has lots of money and knows that's how to get you into bed."

I spun around to find him right at my back. He wasn't angry, at least his face didn't give away if he was. The heat creeping up my neck sent a warning signal to my stomach. Something wasn't right about his demeanor.

"Tell yourself whatever you need to. I'll email you back in the morning." My key turned the deadbolt, and I pushed the door open.

A force shoved me through the entryway, then the

door closed behind me with a rush of wind. Ben's outreached arm barred me to the wall, his hand wrapped around my throat. It was his eyes that gave away the hatred he was acting on.

I struggled for air. My fingernails carved into the back of his hand, trying to pry his grip loose, but he was too strong. This wasn't the first time he'd tried to put me in my place with force. I was transported to the last time he had his hands on me: the night he'd kicked me out of our condo. I'd had to sleep in my car. He'd been upset that I didn't have dinner ready for him at 10 p.m. after he said he'd be home at six.

Unlike that night, Ben didn't reek of alcohol. He was stone-cold sober. The fumes of his eerily calm rage whirled behind his blue irises, and I knew he wasn't going to let me live to see tomorrow.

"Seere," I croaked through his crushing hold.

"Is that his name? The demon you sold your soul to just to watch me lose everything? You should have killed me, Sloane. You should have known that letting me live would come back to bite you in the ass." His low voice was barely registering over the pounding of blood in my ears.

"Seere," I tried again.

I didn't have the trinket that he'd given me. But he'd just been inside of me. That had to have some sort of effect. It had to have heightened that unbreakable bond he always threatened me with.

"He may have destroyed the demon I was working with, but the deal was already done. I won, Sloane. I fought like Hell to get out of the shithole you put me in. The months of rehab. Losing everything I owned to medical bills. My contract lapsing due to injury and poor behavior. No team would touch me as a player. But I still had plenty of buddies willing to sign with me as their agent."

My vision was fading as he rambled. I screamed Seere's name in my head, but there was no sign of him.

"And sure, I had a little help from the demon I found on my own to work with—your old buddy Rick let that slip out during a night of partying. Now I have the upper hand. But you won't be around to see that."

His other hand came up and squeezed over his already vise-like fist.

"Please," I whispered. "Ben, please."

He took a step into me, his arms losing some of their force as they bent so his mouth came close to mine. He took a ragged breath, and I used that moment to strike. My knee connected hard with his groin, and he bent over in pain. I smashed the high heel of my shoe into his knee, then his ribs.

I'd paid close attention to his injury reports.

I kicked off my shoes and sprinted for the stairs. If I could make it to my closet. To the ring . . .

"Bitch!" He roared, and his lumbering body came running after me.

I slammed my bedroom door then shoved the dressing chair in front of the knob. It wouldn't hold, but I didn't wait to see it fail. I darted to my closet, shut the door, and frantically jammed Seere's ring onto my finger.

"Seere, damn it!"

There was a harsh noise in my bedroom. A loud boom of the door being torn from its hinges.

"Fuck." I sucked in a harsh sob and sank to the floor under the rack of hanging clothes.

I felt like a child cowering from an angry parent. He'd caught me in my agreement with Seere. He knew my dirty little secret, and he was going to punish me for not lying down and dying when he wanted me to.

Every muscle in my body wound tight as I waited for what would come next.

Why was the closet door still closed? There wasn't a lock on it, and it was as thin as plywood compared to the one I imagined was now destroyed.

There was a shout, a crash, and another loud bang. Thrashing.

A deadened pounding of one solid mass hitting another came through the space under the door. It sounded like clashing bulls pummeling each other. The door rattled wildly with the impact of something heavy then stopped suddenly. Building up the courage—or panicked urge to run for the hills—I crawled forward. My shaking hand reached for the doorknob and turned it. Through the crack in the door, I could see the small corner of Hell my floor had become.

The wet smack of knuckles on flesh and the sound of cartilage cracking roiled my stomach, but the panic in my chest cut off the projection of vomit threatening my esophagus. The glass-like crunch of teeth and jawbone gave way to a sobbing Ben.

I scrambled to my feet and lunged, screaming Seere's name as I tried and failed to heave him off. Ben was unrecognizable. His nose was bent at a sickening angle. His lips poured blood down his chin and onto his shirt.

If he survived the beating he was getting, he'd be eating from a tube for weeks.

I hooked my arm around Seere's. "Seere, please. Anything. I'll give you anything if you please just stop. You're killing him!"

The command halted Seere's fist mid-swing. His eyes snapped to mine, and his rage melted away to something between relief and shock.

Ben's body fell to the floor in a heap as Seere released his hold to cup my face in his bloodied hands.

The tacky liquid coated my cheek then trailed down to my bruised and aching neck.

"You," Seere whispered. "All I've ever wanted is you."

I choked on the tears I didn't remember starting. "I know."

He pulled us both to our feet. His eyes frantically searched mine. "Say it again." His statement sounded more like a plea. "Sloane. Say. It. Again."

"I'll give you anything."

"Everything." He shook his head slowly, as if he couldn't believe what I'd said. "I *need* everything from you."

I looked at the man who'd tried to kill me wheezing on the floor. He wasn't moving, but his chest was still rising with ragged breaths.

"No." Seere pulled me back to his eyes. "Only me. No one else ever again. Only us."

His stained thumb pushed one of my tears across my hot cheek. We backed up to the edge of my bed, and with a gentle nudge, I lowered to sit. Seere straddled my knees, towering over me with blood smeared across one side of his face. His hair fell over his eyes, adding to the darkness pouring over me.

"Only me?" The question tightened my chest, squeezing my heart. Or my soul. It was already marked for him, no matter how he answered.

"Let me show you what forever feels like."

He pulled his shirt over his head then got to his knees between my legs. His palms pushed my knees apart, and his eyes dropped from mine.

"Fuck," he groaned. He rolled his eyes back with ravishment before looking up at me. "Red lace."

I nodded and pulled my dress off to show him the full crimson set.

He brought his face up to mine, hovering his body over me. Then the world fell away when his lips met mine. I wrapped my arms around his neck, and he dragged me up to the middle of the bed.

The frenzy set in. He wasn't moving fast enough.

My fingers pulled at his belt and pants. The ache in my core and the pounding of my heart couldn't stand another minute of not feeling his skin on mine.

One finger dipped and pulled at the delicate fabric so his tongue could flick my hard nipple. My hips rose in a desperate arch, searching for him, and his free hand obliged. The thong I'd been wearing slipped away, and his fingers made hard circles around my throbbing clit, teasing and building the tension deep in my belly.

"Please," I huffed out.

He looked up at me, releasing my breast. "My little flame, I'm going to give you everything you've ever craved."

The pads of his fingers swept through my arousal, and he brought it up to my lips, pushing inside. I sucked the sweet, slippery taste from his fingers, taking them deeper over my tongue just to drive him wild.

With his sight fused to mine, he took his wet fingertips from my mouth and trailed them down my chest, over my belly then hip. His arm pulled me into him, bringing us into a deep kiss while the head of his cock pressed against my entrance. The thick crown stretched me over him, but he pulled away to keep me on the cusp.

I was caged to the bed by his knees and elbows next to my head. Our breaths collided between us, mine heavy and indigent, his slow and deliberate. His hips pulsed, easing his cock too slowly inside of me. The lines of his face didn't change, but his lips parted to suck the air from my lungs. His face turned, and his eyes demanded I follow until I was forced to realize Ben was still lying on the ground, unconscious.

"Do you see what I would do for you?"

Seere thrust deep. So deep. My gasp met my moan in my throat.

"I will hunt your enemies down and beat them bloody. Then I'll praise this pussy next to their brutalized corpses."

His pace hardened.

The tops of his thighs slapped against me as he

drove into me harder and faster. The building orgasm in my core intensified when he looked at me. "You think I'm bloodthirsty now. But make me your assassin and the world will burn at your feet."

A clash of emotions and his relentless hips sent me over the edge, and I plummeted into ecstasy. My head fell back onto the soft duvet while every nerve in my body lit up just for him in a show of appreciation and acceptance of the promises he'd always kept.

Our hoarse moans of pleasure echoed around us. Seere gripped my shoulder and thigh tightener. His heavy breath hit my chest. Every thrust became shorter, more rigid, until he stilled, cum gushing and filling me deep.

My lungs fought for air but couldn't draw it in fast enough to keep up with my heart. Seere buried his face between my breasts. His sweet kisses over my sensitive flesh masked the hunger I knew still coursed through him. He would always be starved. Until our souls fused together at the end of time, we would never be close enough.

There was a shuddering grunt from Ben. His hands twitched, then he rolled his head from one side to the other.

Seere withdrew from me and got to his feet. He tugged his pants up around his waist and pulled a blade from some unseen place. He walked around Ben's body, grabbed him by the scruff of his neck, then held the sharp instrument to Ben's throat.

Ben's grotesque, bloodshot eyes flitted open.

Seere's gaze locked with mine. "Are you done with him?"

Words flooded my brain, but what spoke the loudest was Seere's promise: "*. . . the moment you tire of watching him dangle on the hook, I would rip him apart . . .*"

I swallowed. The painful pull of muscles there reminded me of what Ben would have done if I hadn't fought like Hell.

I was always the one fighting for redemption. Always having to prove that I was worthy of success, worthy of the life I'd built with my two hands.

I might have wished for Ben to suffer, but I'd climbed out of my grief to the top of my field.

"You should have killed me, Sloane. You should have known that letting me live would come back to bite you in the ass."

I let my chin fall. Just once.

Seere sliced through flesh, cartilage, and bone.

My prince of carnage.

My constant demon.

My Seere.

How did you get this number?

I have my sources.

Send me a picture.

Did you lose your mind while I was gone?

Contract

e or Your Company's Name]
ne 1]
ne 2]
Zip Code]

ame or Company's Name]
]
Code]

e or Heading**

greement") is made and entered into on [Date], between [Your Na... ...pany's Name] ("Party A") and
or Company's Name] ("Party B").

or objective of the agreement in clea...

ons:**

itions, and resp...   terms,

CHAPTER 14
SEERE

I sent Sloane to shower while I cleaned Ben from her carpets. Aside from the blood on her cheeks and hips, she was relatively unscathed, but she didn't need to see the process. It was better that I took Ben's body to Hell and used magic to hide the rest of the evidence.

When I was done, I stripped my clothes off, sent them through the void, and entered her bathroom. Steam filled the room, fogging the mirror and glass shower walls, but I could still make out her silhouette.

She was already through washing herself when I stepped inside. The clean, fruity scent of her shampoo surrounded me as I moved into her. I looked at the finger-shaped bruises forming around her neck. The outline of where Ben had not only touched what was mine but had attempted to take her from me brought fire to my chest.

Pounding my fists into his face and slicing his throat had been too quick. I should have dragged it out. Chained him to a cold slab in my basement and tortured him for days. Sliced into his flesh, burned him with a red-hot iron, let his wounds fester until he begged for death. Only then would I have bled him dry while he watched me fuck Sloane in every hole that I owned.

It was too late for that. But the next human to cross her would bear that fate.

She moved out of the stream of water and pushed me into it. Her gaze followed the rust-colored river that ran from my body, over the floor, and finally down the drain. I poured soap into my hand and washed away the only remains of Ben on this plane. He'd be considered a missing person until a few of the demons we'd placed on the police force got word of the real story. His case would run cold within a week. I'd make sure of that.

I scrubbed the suds of shampoo out of my hair. Sloane was somber. If she was upset or regretful, it didn't show. We could have broken the tension with words, but instead, I smoothed my hands over the soft skin of her forearms then picked up her wrists and pinned them over her head to the wall behind her.

Her lips pursed then parted. But her eyes passed from mine to my lips then back again. The soft blush of her cheeks sent blood pulsing to my cock. Every other thought died away to reveal a single motivation: my sole purpose was to be buried in this woman for as many hours a day as I could be. I would lay siege to the world just to ensure that she had no other duty but to fuck me. If I couldn't be inside of her this instant, what use was there to breathe or exist?

I lowered my lips to hers and waited for permission. Waited to see if I'd finally earned the prize behind the years of her rejection. Would maiming and murdering in her name be proof enough that I was wholly her monster to command?

She drew in a long breath, closed her eyes, and dived into the metaphoric deep end. This was no brazen, feverish kiss, but a lascivious, sweltering one that drove into the far reaches of my putrid soul. A moan of relief passed from her throat to mine as our tongues languidly coiled together. I let her hands free so her fingers could weave into my hair and mine could cup her cheeks.

I rolled my hips, and my excitement coated her slick belly. One of her hands came to wrap around my shaft. The first pumps were slow and deliberate. Down to my base then up to the tip. Again and again.

She smiled against my lips when I groaned my impatience.

"Do you love me, Seere?" Her sultry voice pulled me farther under the spell she was casting.

Bending low to plant a kiss to the sensitive spot at her hip that always made her squirm, I pulled her body up the wall. Her legs wrapped around my waist, and I looked into her eyes so I knew she would not just hear my words, but see the truth in them.

"Love you?" I lined up the head of my cock to her wet heat. "No, Sloane. What I have for you has no comparison to love."

Her mouth slackened as I eased her down my shaft.

"I was created, fought, survived, and yearned just so that I could be yours."

I thrust into her. Her head lolled against the wall, and my mouth sucked at the beads of water at her throat.

"Seere!" she cried out. "Oh fuck."

"Do you love me, Sloane?"

"Please."

The wet slap of her ass on the tile drowned out her answer.

"Do you love me, little flame?"

"Yes!"

She pulled my face up to hers, kissing me deeply, relentlessly as I rutted inside of her.

"I love you," she mewled. "Fuck, I love you. I love you."

My balls tightened. The mounting release curled in my core, and her name rattled in my chest as my cum covered her pulsating inner walls. Her pussy tightened around me, and her scream of pleasure bounced around the bathroom.

I pumped inside of her once. Twice. Until she dripped with my essence.

Her muscles weakened around my neck and waist. Instead of helping her stand, I scooped her into my chest. Reaching over to the tap, I shut it off and walked us out to her bedroom. There was no need for a towel. I wasn't done fucking what was finally and admittedly mine.

Sloane gazed up at me through hooded eyes. "You're mine?"

"I'm yours."

Forever.

Messages on phone:
- How did you get this number?
- I have my sources.
- Send me a picture.
- Did you lose your mind while I was gone?

Contract

[e or Your Company's Name]
[ne 1]
[e 2]
[Zip Code]

[me or Company's Name]
[ ]
[Code]

[or Heading]

[greement") is made and entered into on [Date], between [Your Na...
[er Company's Name] ("Party B").

[or objective of the agreement in clea... ...pany's Name] ("Party A") and

[ons:]

[tions, and se... ...terms.

CHAPTER 15
SLOANE

Seere sat at the foot of my bed, watching me get dressed for work. We hadn't slept. I didn't know if sleep deprivation for a demon was really a concern, but I was beyond tired. He hadn't relented. Hour after hour, we fucked, sucked, and came more times than I could remember.

The shower I'd taken when my alarm went off washed away the fluids we'd exchanged, but it did nothing to wake me up. I wanted more than anything to sleep. But since I knew it would arouse suspicion if I didn't go to work the day that Ben was realized to be missing, I dressed to kill.

I wore my favorite turtleneck dress and spent extra time covering the bruises, hickeys, and bite marks left from the night before.

When I put the final touches of perfume on my

wrists, Seere wrapped his arms around my chest, enveloping me in musk, sex, and lust.

"Let's go to Napoli," he said with a kiss to my jaw.

"I have to work."

"Tonight, then." His arms banded my ass to his hips, making his thick erection known.

I spun around in his arms to wrap mine around his neck. The freedom to show him affection was becoming less of an internal struggle. Fighting off these feelings for so long while he chased me had only made it harder to demolish the walls I'd built after Ben had dumped me.

I looked into Seere's eyes and knew he was waiting to see if I would push him away again. "I want to go to Morocco."

The hard lines of his face eased into a wicked smile that turned my insides to jelly. "I will fuck you in any city you want."

"Now you don't mind if I run off to faraway places?"

"You can't run from me anymore, spitfire. You promised me your heart last night, which means I have you. Heart, body, and soul."

I pushed up to my toes and kissed his soft, full lips. The remnants of our night together still clung to them and sent a flutter of goose bumps over my skin.

"You love me." I held his gaze through my lashes,

knowing the chances of me getting to the office on time were getting thinner by the second.

A deep rumble came from his chest. "If I say those words, will you stay here and let me fuck you to sleep?"

My teeth tugged on my lip as I shook my head. "No. But there's a good chance I'll let you eat me out under my desk later if you say it."

He threw his head back and cursed my name. "You're killing me, little flame."

I pulled at the back of his neck until his eyes returned to mine.

"You. Love. Me." I dotted every word with a quick kiss on his pouty lips.

His playful smile pulled into a solemn smirk. "I love you. Brighter than every star that ever shined, darker than any darkness that ever existed. I. Love. You."

THE END
For now…

Light my Fire, Baby

1 oz Spicy Tamarind Vodka

1 oz Simple Syrup

0.5 oz Lime Juice

Chili Candy Powerder for the rim

Garnish with a slice of candied Jalapeño and slice of lime

IF YOU'VE MADE IT THIS FAR... WOW!

We made it!

I don't know if someone told me at a weird point in my life that I couldn't do amazing things, but no one is more proud of this accomplishment than me.

This series was a culmination of over a year of studying mythology, demonology, witchcraft, occult, and the metaphysical to create a world worth getting lost in.

When I set out to write the Seven Deadly Sins, it all started with Sitri. The lust demon who would not leave me alone, and screamed for his own story. I'm so glad I listened.

As the series went on, each prince made himself at home in my soul. I couldn't pick a favorite because they all have a part of me that they will always refuse to give back. Which makes me love them even more.

I hope that you've enjoyed this ride and will come with me to the next great adventure. There are so many great stories to come, but these boys will always be alive in my heart.

ACKNOWLEDGMENTS

As always, I have to thank my editing team for the magic they turn my manuscripts into. It really does take remarkable people to make a good story great.

I'm constantly amazed by the readers who not only enjoy my work, but tell their friends and fellow smut lovers. As much as I want to scream from the rooftops about my books, I could never do it as passionately as my readers have. Thank you so much!

To every one of my writing friends who watched me write and release this series in one year but thought I was nuts. You're right, I was. But your support made it possible. Your encouragement has meant the world to me <3

On to another adventure! I can't wait to see what happens next.